John MacNair Reid was born in Glasgow in 1895, and worked as a journalist with the *Glasgow Herald*, and in later years with the *Inverness Courier*, the Glasgow *Evening Times* and *Evening News*.

In 1936 his wife Josephine, a medical Doctor, took a job with the Highlands and Islands Medical Service, and Reid went free-lance. They lived in Eigg until the War, which Reid spent in Glasgow, and after the War moved first to Laggan, Inverness-shire, and then Torridon in Wester Ross. Reid died in 1954, as a result of an accident. During his lifetime he published, as well as *Homeward Journey*, two books of poetry, *Symbols* and *The Gleam on the Road*, and edited a volume of *Scottish Short Stories*. Two further novels, *Tobias the Rod* and *Judy From Crown Street* were issued posthumously.

John MacNair Reid

HOMEWARD JOURNEY

Introduced by J. B. Pick

'The homeward journey to habitual self'
KEATS

CANONGATE
CLASSICS
13

First published in 1934 by Porpoise Press
This edition first published as a Canongate Classic in 1988
by Canongate Publishing Limited
17 Jeffrey Street
Edinburgh EH1 1DR

Canongate Classics
Series Editor: Roderick Watson
Editorial Board: Tom Crawford, J.B. Pick

British Library Cataloguing in Publication Data

Reid, John MacNair.
Homeward journey.—(Canongate classics).
I. Title
823'.912[F]

ISBN 0–86241–178–5

The publishers gratefully acknowledge
general subsidy from the Scottish Arts Council
towards the Canongate Classics series
and a specific grant towards the
publication of this volume

Set by Falcon Graphic Art Ltd, Wallington, Surrey
Cover printed by Wood Westworth, St. Helen's
Printed and bound in Great Britain
by Cox and Wyman, Reading

Contents

Introduction

This book takes its place with Willa Muir's *Imagined Corners* and the novels of Nan Shepherd as works forgotten or neglected not because of any failings they may have, but because in the nineteen-thirties, that heyday of best-sellers and Book Society Choices, they were unobtrusive in their honesty of purpose, and made no grand gestures. This is a quiet book, but not a gentle one, remarkable for strength and clarity of organisation, and the relentless subtelty of its insight. The structure is oddly formal, with each part fulfilling the function of one Act in a play. And yet the novel aims not at all at drama, but at psychological truth, and subordinates everything to that end.

The story is in outline simple, in detail complex: a young man haunted by the death of his mother tries to break free with a night on the town, and falls immediately into a relationship with the first girl he meets. But this is in no ordinary sense a love story. The book charts with delicate precision an association between two people who are deserts apart in culture, upbringing, aspirations, attitudes and temperament, and based from the start upon concealment and deception on both sides: 'When he asked her questions about her home it did not occur to her to tell the truth.' David could be seen as a sensitive manipulator trying to force Jessie into his mother's mould, and Jessie as a charming predator seeking to use David to escape from a feckless father and a bed-ridden mother. But this bald description would not do justice to the closely-observed reality of both characters, who grow and change as we read, revealed through continual shifts in point of view. David does not accept Jessie's need to escape; but we can. Jessie does not understand why she fails with men; but we do. This is a measure of the book's authenticity.

The reader may ask himself 'Who was right?' and give his own answer. Reid retains his balance and makes no judgement, but my own suspicion is that David's peculiar form of self-consciousness has in it an element of perverseness, while Jessie's practical selfishness is a form of integrity fundamental to survival.

Although modest in scope, *Homeward Journey* has large general themes moving below the surface: the nature of moral perception, the decline of religious belief, the effects of spiritual poverty.

> 'Do you think Calvinism is dead?'
> 'I don't know. Do you?'
> 'I think it served its purpose. But if we don't watch we may deserve another scourge like it.'

David has been deeply influenced by his mother's fastidious ethics. To his office colleagues he seems a prig: 'The modern indictment of Puritanism was directed against him by men of an honest depravity.' This idea of 'honest depravity', of man as naturally amoral, is contrasted with David's continual discriminations—whether out of refinement or ethics is open to question. The office man-of-the-world, Clifford, tells him 'I'll make a man of you in a single night.' But afterwards David feels 'The night-life of Clifford's had poisoned him with its tastes and smells.'

Jessie seems at first to symbolise sexual freedom, then David is charmed by her 'decency', and at last she becomes the object of his moral pressure. At one point it is said: 'They've an idea that the whole system of moral responsibility and decency is contained in religion or a church. So if you don't go to church you don't respond to or recognise the system.' But what, if not a church and its doctrines, justifies the system? Reid does not answer this question specifically, but in a sense the whole book is an examination of the basis for individual moral judgement. My own feeling is that the logic of denying authority would force him either into ethical agnosticism or into acceptance of the extreme Protestant doctrine of the 'inner light'. But only continual awareness of motive, and the deepest attention to the discoveries of an insight at once personal and objective, can prevent this doctrine from leading to self-deception. And in fact it is the self-deceptions of David and Jessie with which the novel deals so carefully. Neither protagonist faces the fundamental assumptions by which they live, and we are left to draw our own conclusions about their particular moral attitudes and about ethical judgement in general.

John Macnair Reid's models were Continental—he had some of the subtelty of Proust—but his preoccupations were essentially Scottish. Certainly he combined the qualities of the poet and the novelist, and those who read *Homeward Journey* with sympathy will recognise him for the talented and significant writer he was—scrupulous, truthful and accurate.

J.B.Pick

PART ONE

The Mother

She died during their childhood, and when they came to talk placidly about her David always recalled her by some phrase she had used. There was more of her memory than this, of course; but he was strangely secretive about the rest. There were things he had said to her and looks they had exchanged which remained as vivid as her words. These were hidden and private. But her memory had a public side, and from it he could draw as liberally as other members of the family. His father, the minister, liked to hear him tell of the idea she had given him during Temperance Week, and had even used the story in the pulpit. 'What are you going to be, my little man?' was the silly question many people were putting to David, and his mother's suggestion as his reply was 'A teetotaler!' He caught on to the idea at once and was gratified by the way it made people laugh. Everyone thought it very neat for a minister's son during the Week.

Mrs Carruthers put all sorts of ideas for daily conduct into the boy's head, and her manner of pretending to be serious made the fun of it all unforgettable. She had a grip on him from the beginning. When he came home from school she often smiled at his eagerness to tell her of what he had seen or heard. His two sisters, Elizabeth and Jane, gave her newsy minutes at bedtime; but their talk, though of the atmosphere of the house, could have been culled from the chatter in hundreds of Glasgow nurseries. David's little titbits impressed by their obvious relevancy. He recounted what he had seen or thought when he knew her to be personally interested. Thus it was that he came to her one evening and said, 'Mother, if you go now to the garden, you'll see your red cloud.' She went out, and there it was, last and lonely in a sky of twilight fragility and not the stretch of a bird's wings from the half-moon still frozen in daylight. They watched it till it drifted behind the red tenements of Crosshill. 'And why do you say it's my red cloud, darling?' she asked him. 'I mean, it's like the one you liked the last time,' he replied. One other evening he came to her and said he had been unhappy all day because he had taken the outside piece of the brown loaf at breakfast although he knew she liked it best. At this she ruffled his hair and sent him chasing.

David remembered these things in after days, and felt a warm glow as he contemplated what they meant. He was glad to think he had behaved nicely toward her, and he fancied she had often, especially near the end, given him hints of her appreciation of his tenderness.

His sisters, remarking on minor differences in their mother's treatment of them, found a ready explanation in his sex. In this they were supported by their father, who teased his wife about it. But he too was proud of his son David, and glad to have him strong and healthy, since a cruel fate had robbed him of two other boys, Sinclair, their first-born, and Thomas, their last. To the children Sinclair was but a name that brought a sadness to their mother's eyes; but Tom had lived long enough to be remembered vividly as someone audacious enough to die.

The time came when their number was complete and the family rhyme, given by their mother one golden evening in the garden, summed up their little history:

> Sinclair came first and went away,
> Betty came next and stayed;
> Sinclair came back another day,
> This time we called him David.

> Jane was the youngest for two years
> And then came Thomas Bain;
> But he was quick to bring our tears,
> Jane was the youngest again.

It was a Sunday evening, church was long over and they were idling in the dusk, loath to go indoors. Someone had asked who this Sinclair was that they all heard about, and Mrs Carruthers turned and put a hand on David's head saying simply, 'David; but he forgot to bring something God left out for him, and so he had to go back.'

'Then, am I really the eldest?' cried David, seeing a new distinction.

'Oh no. If a baby makes a mistake he loses his chance and has to begin all over again. You took so long looking for the thing you had forgotten that Betty was here before you, and so she's the oldest of you all.'

'What was it I forgot, mother?' David then inquired eagerly.

'Why, my little man,' laughed his father, who had enjoyed this somewhat unorthodox fable, 'surely you are the one to tell us that!'

David lived to regret his father's interruption. But for that he might have had his mother's answer to complete the story.

Then, taking little Jane on her knee and smiling to her husband, she recited those verses which gave them their chronological list. That was the summer before she died.

She gave them no warning. She went out one afternoon and did not come back. The minister, who behaved strangely in a mood of surviving tenderness, told the children she had gone to live with a friend in town for a few days. As the owner of the nursing-home was a member of the congregation, this was the bare skeleton of the truth which the children had subsequently to clothe with their own imaginings. After the

stipulated few days the coffin was brought home and waited
two nights and a day until the funeral to Cathcart Cemetery.

David bore his grief 'like a little man' as the minister said.
He cried sorely at night and again in the morning if his sisters infected him with tears, but he resumed school the day
after the funeral and took to his lessons as doggedly as ever.
He remembered the story of a beautiful lady who was never
known to smile after her lover died, and he wondered what
remark or what sight would make him smile his first smile after his mother's death. And if he did smile, would that mean
that he did not love his mother as fondly as the beautiful lady
had loved her lover? The suggestion filled him with shame.
Knowing, however, that he was bound to smile some time,
he went to her portrait in the dining-room and smiled up to
her. Then his eyes filled with tears.

She was gone; but from the first there was no hint that
she was really dead to him. He admitted her death when
faced by the essential and trivial affairs of every day, and
accepted without a challenge the rearrangements in a familiar house now organized to continue without her. But that he
had lost her never occurred to him. The sense of loss was to
awaken after many years, when boyhood was over.

Being in a minister's house, there was the minimum of
religious consolation. Instinctively the children, and particularly David, sought other ways of fortifying the heart
against the pain of desolation and that vague apprehension
of personal violence children experience in a house of death.
The illusions David built for himself were made by material
gathered from his mother rather than from his father, for
the mother-material was simpler and made memorable by
her charm, whereas the familiar symbols of his father had to
be memorized for church whether one understood them or
not. Moreover, his father had a particular speech for church
which never varied and which was gladly suspended as soon
as he got home. David came to believe that everything spoken in that ministerial voice didn't matter a jot.

But his mother had had no second voice, the use of which was a sign she was speaking rot. She was always the same, meaning everything she said, and giving a topic something of her charm which made its association with her inevitable afterwards. She had had a quiet authoritative air, controlling their little world with an ease that made it appear leisured and endless. While the minister was apt to perplex them with his biblical allusions, she with toys and dresses and suits, school-lessons and friends, holidays and work, reduced the vastness of the world to a scale they could comprehend.

When she was gone they had to keep what they could of the shape of old days. But it was conscious imitation, and children tire of imitation however prone they are to it. Soon the time came when little restrictions she had imposed were cautiously scrutinized. One of these concerned the ivy that had once clung to the wall around the small side window of the big room. Mrs Carruthers had disapproved of ivy; it created damp in the wintertime and flies in the summer, and withal she considered it unlucky. She had it removed. But the children secretly admired ivy-clad walls farther along the avenue, and their mother was not long dead when they persuaded Richard, the church officer, to restore the plant below the 'ivy window' of their drawing-room.

They found this the more easy, both with Richard and their conscience, on account of the support given them by Mrs MacKinlay, the housekeeper their father had engaged to look after them. Anything connected with the garden was sympathetically treated by Mrs MacKinlay, who in her fondness for it soon allowed the house indoors to suffer for its sake. She would rather have flower beds tidy than bedroom beds, because, as she might laughingly admit, the minister's visitors didn't see the bedrooms. They didn't see the children's cupboards either, or their chest-of-drawers where their clothes had once been arranged in dependable orderliness. Mrs MacKinlay never had socks and stockings washed and darned at regular intervals, nor handkerchiefs washed and ironed and laid away in neat little files in the drawers. The need for a blowing of noses became as unpleasant as the discovery of a hole in the heel of a sock.

Those early days of Mrs MacKinlay's dispensation occupied in David's memory a corner of silence. During her first days in the manse the minister told the children that she might feel the loneliness of her position were they to discuss someone who had dominated their affections in a manner she could never hope to achieve, and that it would be a kindness to refrain from speaking of their mother before her. David, at least, had no inclination to speak of his mother to anyone then. It was months later, when the pains of dismemberment had eased somewhat, that the restriction was felt. But whereas he came to see his mother sublimated by this extreme reticence, the girls had the awkward notion that speaking of her anywhere was in bad taste. It was like speaking in church, especially the manse pew of the church. Elizabeth once recalled a method her mother had of tying a parcel, and the parcel, in the process of being tied at the time, was taken away from her. There was a look on her father's face then which implied that she was guilty of some maidenly indiscretion. In such a Christian home it was not right to speak casually about someone who was dead.

Observing this, David was not quite sure what to make of it. He went into the dining-room and stood looking up at the portrait. He expected to feel embarrassed, he wanted to feel embarrassed, and yet he was not. There was no stifling, freezing atmosphere in the room now; everything was normal. And so it came about for him that only when he was emotionally exalted could he summon his mother's memory with anything like reality, and always it was in the secrecy of his own heart. As time wore on that summons was made by ever more and more subtle and fugitive signals.

Signals? What were they? When he was first made aware

of death by the absence of Tom, who died when he was four, David went about the nursery touching things and whispering to himself, 'Tommy touched these once,' and trying hard, oh so hard, to realize something, he scarcely knew what. He supposed it was his method of testing the depth of death's mystery. His spirit was listening for some response from the things Tommy had touched, as though he had let a stone fall into a dark well and was waiting an echo from the far away. But that was no use now. There was no speculative touching of things his mother had known. He avoided things too closely associated with her. The signals that brought her back were seldom if ever physical; they were little incalculable tricks of the mind.

He went through boyhood with these as his only spiritual experience. They were not tricks that he could have mentioned at home, and least of all could he have mentioned them to his father. The minister was a good man and a kindly father, yet when he died he passed into the memory as a sensuous man unlikely to have appreciated any form of spiritual excitement. When he was gone, David at the age of twenty-one could not think of him out of the flesh. His face never came swimmingly upon a grey mist, filling up one's vision and soaking into one's consciousness. That was how his mother came on responding to his summons. When he recalled his father he thought of a tobacco-pouch and pipe, a book-wrap, collar-stud, secretive button-fastener, paper-knife and opaque snuff-box. Serving his father, these little things had seemed controlled, as occasional glances at Mrs MacKinlay, by a mind that knew exactly their uses in the routine of life. Now lying unheeded in odd corners, to be come upon unexpectedly and left with hazy sentiment, they were pitiable, humiliated little things, while the manner of glancing at Mrs MacKinlay was only remembered when the whole man was pictured sitting at his ease or passing through the kitchen to the stairs. With him death had been a destroyer as savage as a beast in the jungle.

It had always been so with his father. When he was ill, as he frequently was during his last five years, David went in dread lest his sensory enjoyment should be ended. Recovering from a bout of bronchitis was the minister's most pleasant time. The cares of the church devolved on someone else, and Sundays merged into other days of the week and evened out a long period of comfort. In his bed he kept a bundle of books, which were changed every few days from the library, and an ashtray made out of a porringer, on which his pipes and pouch and matches were at hand. How he loved to lie there and read and smoke, safe in the warm blankets! And when returning spring found him well again, David's heart was a tumult of rejoicing. 'See, he is all right! The present is far inland yet!' In the end, so aware was he of his father's life, death caught him unawares.

When his father died it was as though his mother was bereaved. He behaved as a son should, and his grief was real and lasting. Yet he was self-conscious in it, and when he thought of his mother there was a perceptible cringing as though he feared her wrath for some omission of love. His apprehension of her, started in this way, grew until the day arrived when if the thought of her came to him acutely—and it seemed to rush in upon him without warning—he cried out, no matter where he was.

His mind at such a time was pandemonium behind his frontal calm. When the thing happened he involuntarily cried out. But he was quick enough to control the cry so that it seemed to come from some normal passage of thought. He might be sitting with his sisters at a meal, or in a restaurant with someone, or walking with a friend; suddenly the jab would come and his mind leap like a body pinked by a sword. 'But I say—!' he would cry, or 'Yes, yes, yes, of course!' or 'But I don't understand—'; something that was not impossible to the topic at the moment. The conversation would swing on it haltingly and then resume. If he was alone the thing ended in a self-conscious laugh.

One winter's night he was in the big room alone. The lamp was on the table beside the ivy window and his chair was backed to it and close against a crackling fire. His sister Elizabeth was in a room upstairs entertaining some friends, and he was at leisure with a book when he broke his pipe. It snapped in the middle, leaving a small piece of vulcanite, rough-edged, within the wooden stem. In disgust he threw both pieces into the fire.

It was the only pipe he possessed, and he was on the point of going out to buy a new one when the thought occurred, with a brief anticipatory thrill, that he might use one of his father's. He went over to the desk at the other window and searched for a brown briar of which his father had been very fond. There it was in his hand, a bit of wood with incommunicable memories. It was dusty. A tiny cluster of charred ashes was stuck fast to the foot of the bowl. He scraped with his knife and then raised the stem to his lips. But halfway he hesitated, looked at it again and, unscrewing the vulcanite, walked through to the bathroom, where he rinsed the mouthpiece under the hot-water tap.

The odour of stale nicotine rose in the steam, and the mirror above the basin was immediately clouded. Suddenly her face swam in to him with the stealth of a shadow and the swiftness of a lightning flash. His mind staggered behind it. He dropped his pipe and shrieked at her, 'I didn't mean to slight him: it was dusty with lying so long!'

When Elizabeth came running from the stairs he was singing. 'Idiot!' she said, 'you nearly frightened us out of our wits!'

For many days Elizabeth told the story to visitors, and David helped by looking like a man who, even when not in the bath, sings in the bathroom. But he knew now that the mechanism of resistance was giving way and that his mind had an exposed place which must not be touched. Yet he kept edging on it as the tongue tentatively dares the exposed nerve of a tooth.

He was engrossed in the most homely and innocent affairs. A fortnight's tranquillity would give him confidence, and he would laugh and say it was all nonsense. To prove its nothingness he would edge closer than before in a blustering way, like a reckless youth showing off before children. But he soon realized that such insolence would never summon her and would only make the next visitation more terrible to bear. He could not be insolent all the while; he was powerless against a return to normality.

And so it grew on him in spite of everything, and might have lasted for long enough had not Uncle James unwittingly come to the rescue. Uncle James, who was his mother's brother, had always been the hard, efficient man of business. He was the economic adviser, the financial rock of the family. This position was the hall-mark of success for one who had learned early that efficiency and a show of hardness were features of the business man as much as a bowler hat, and natural tenderness and credulity had been submerged by an affectation of pertness that ultimately encrusted the man's character. In an ordinary social encounter, however, he was tolerable enough. He was sane in the world's affairs, and he was dependable. When David and Elizabeth, on their father's death, were left alone in Cornfoot Avenue (Jane being by this time married), Uncle James took on himself the responsibility of looking in on them, and his quiet confidence and efficient air helped to steady them. He drained their affairs of sentiment. 'I'm really their guardian now,' he told his business friends, and he loved the sound of the word. He got David into a coalmaster's office in town and had some practical talks with Elizabeth about her shop. These were things he could do, and he seemed genuinely pleased about them.

The visits of such a man were regulated and in the nature of occasions. He did not actually 'drop in', though that was the phrase he used. He came at tea-time or at lunch-time on Sunday, when the necessary function of a meal could be attended in this house as readily as anywhere else. Thus he saved time.

He spoke of stocks and shares, of his family's education, of the house at Tayvallich that he had taken for the summer, or of the theatre shows he wanted to see during the winter. He rarely encouraged his niece and nephew to speak of themselves, and six months after their father's death decided that there was no occasion to speak of him any more. It was not the restriction of shyness which embarrassed him: it was the futility of any more discussion. The man was dead.

This attitude was obvious enough to David for months and months, and yet it exercised no influence at all upon him. It was merely Uncle James. But one evening a passing sigh from his uncle did what years of shallow conduct had failed to do. Uncle James's car was at the gate, and when he had been persuaded to wait for tea—more than half of a formality—he said to David that they would go out and switch off the engine. As they were passing the open dining-room door he slackened somewhat and peered inside. Something had caught his eye. 'Aha,' he sighed, and stopped; 'there's poor Mary there. Poor Mary!' He shook his head and passed on.

It was the first time David had heard his uncle speak thus in a voice that was not sad but artificially subdued. Uncle James seemed to be reviving something in his mind which he let go again as soon as the outside door was opened and the sunshine rushed upon him. The world was full of sounds: the indiscriminate noise of distant traffic with the transcendent jangle of a tram in Victoria Road, the agitation of the birds in the garden. It was a busy, pleasant world. The air was cool and sweet.

David felt the years between him and his mother lengthen out to the extent of his uncle's sigh. She had died so long ago. She was dead, as far as sensible Uncle James was concerned, for evermore. The motor-car became at a click silent. But all the other noises continued and the birds chirruped ceaselessly in the garden.

He looked at his uncle intently yet incredulously. 'Was it so?' his heart asked, and there was panic in the words as a freedom of the spirit seemed to open out before him. It was as though his uncle's words, 'Poor Mary!' had knocked a hole in his mind through which the airiness and the sounds of the outside world came in on him.

When they were seated in the big room he was still conscious of the birds and the noise outside, while his uncle's voice made the room vibrate like a busy place. And Elizabeth, in her white frock, with smiling lips and pleasant eyes, was going from kitchen to dining-room and waving to them from the hall. His uncle and he might have been mourners returned from a funeral after which the spring air, the familiar noises of the town and the smell of good food was restoring the mind to its normal level. The quick and the living were comforting themselves.

Tea was soon ready and he sat at his usual place with his back to the window. The birds were fluttering about the shrubs in the garden and upon the lawn behind him. Beyond was the outside world from which Uncle James came with his fine control of sentiment, his air of prosperity and ease. And fashioned into the wall, beside the fireplace, his mother's portrait rose, remote and undisturbing. Times had changed so greatly since her day that she was almost a stranger looking out on this scene, a stranger who had once been the sister, poor Mary, of this complete stranger, Uncle James. The intimacy of her 'visitations' had been a mere trick of the mind practised upon himself.

PART TWO

The Children

Elizabeth and David were now alone in the manse, attended by a young housekeeper, Maisie, a niece of the late Mrs MacKinlay. Their house, however, was no longer a manse save by the endowment of ecclesiastical memories. It was a solid stone-built house with a number VIII elaborately engraved on its rounded pillars at the gate, standing on the crest of the hilly Cornfoot Avenue, which rises from Langside Road, Queen's Park, and dips gently into Crosshill, on the south side of Glasgow. While the minister lived the church had paid the rent and so it was called the manse. But it was not church property. It had belonged to two elderly ladies of the congregation who, as soon as the Rev. Joseph Carruthers died, showed some desire to be the landladies of the new minister. David and Elizabeth had then been faced with losing their home and their birthplace or accepting the alternative of buying. Uncle James was consulted, and after days of cogitation, first by them and then by the old ladies, their offer to purchase was made and accepted, and the manse became a private house in Cornfoot Avenue.

They were quite determined that it should be a private house. For a time after their father's death members of the congregation came visiting, saying it was a house of memories for them. If that was so, how much more a house of memories was it for these children! Unpleasant memories, too, such as were to be erased as quickly as possible: memories of members of the congregation cluttering it up. These people had come at all hours, nosing around and compiling lists for gossip. Elders, deacons, managers and common-or-garden members—they were all alike. So they had to be discouraged.

Elizabeth soon felt the effects of the discouragement in her business. She was an expert needlewoman, and her shop in Grantley Street was the resort of the discerning southside ladies. But members of the congregation whose feelings were hurt refused to patronize the shop and went elsewhere for their blouses and knickers. Elizabeth noted the drop in her receipts as due to her deliberate policy at home, and felt pleased. Her receipts would stand the blow: she could no longer stand the congregation.

Yet many of these people she now set out to rebuff had once admired her greatly. She was the eldest of the family, two years older than David, and when a child she had been the loveliest of them all. She had sung at soirées, at sacred concerts, and latterly in the choir, and many of the social duties given over to the minister's wife devolved upon her. Not a few families in the congregation had blessed her for consignments of eggs and butter and legs of mutton, and sometimes she had gone to bed wondering if she were really Elizabeth Carruthers or some practising character from one of the cheap novelettes. The young men who attended Bible Class or the Literary Society told their weekday friends that the church wasn't so bad a place after all when the minister's daughter could dance superbly and in her chat refer to football-players and prominent sportsmen like a man. She was free and happy with these young men. But that might have been a mere suppleness of the spirit. As the minister's daughter she had to be bland to everyone, and it was more agreeable to be bland to young men than to old ones.

The one surprise she occasioned the church was when she allowed Jane, her young sister, to get married in it before her. Surprise was the general tone when the congregation heard of Jane's wedding: but Elizabeth did not seem to notice. Jane was going to marry Archie Duke, who had jeweller's shop in Sauchiehall Street, and Elizabeth's great task was to find some present—apart from the usual tea-service it was her duty to give—that Archie would not be able to say he could have got through the wholesale. She thought of it for a while, and then her fingers became busy and she produced one of the loveliest pieces of needlework the congregation had ever seen. (For of course the bride's presents were publicly exhibited in the manse at an At Home a few days before the wedding.)

It was a linen teacloth of delicate cream, and sewn upon it, in letters of exquisite form, was the family rhyme learned from her mother in the long ago. The last line

    Jane was the youngest again

was given in German script, and below, making the substance of a dot, were the words, 'My own italics'. It started a fashion that brought a rush of work to the shop and kept her sitting up to all hours for weeks after the wedding.

When she noticed a change upon her brother she decided that he was in love. She would soon be alone. What then, she wondered, would happen? Might she stay on in the manse? No, she couldn't do that, not if David elected to stay there, and she felt it only right that he should. She would require a small flat somewhere near the shop where she could do for herself. Something would turn up. The chief interest meantime was that David was in love.

'You are very cheery these days, David. Is there anything particularly nice happening?' she asked him one night on the way home from a theatre.

'I suppose I'm growing up.'

'Oh yes; falling in love with someone, I suppose.'

'What about a bet on who'll be first?' he suggested.

'No. I'm not tempting Providence in that way.'

Now he could have told her, David thought. It would have been simple to slip from this easy banter which had its source in good feeling into a whisper about something locked in a reserve more tender still. But a tramcar crowded with chattering people was not the proper place for it, and when they reached home the mood was gone. Soon they were separated for the night.

While undressing he speculated on how he would have been feeling had he told her. Rather sheepish, probably, and a good bit lonelier. He imagined vividly her look, her occasional question, the slight rise of an eyebrow. She would have remained normal, nodding her head and saying something about being glad it was all over. Then she would have gone to her bed in the usual way, leaving his little reserve, this little portion of tenderness he preserved from the past, exposed to the light and instant deterioration. Now, he thought, standing near the bed with his trousers upended, their legs flattened together and ready to be placed underneath the mattress, now, if ever, his mother's face should come illumining his mind and her wordless voice fill his inner hearing with reproof. But all was silent and serene. He put away the trousers for their nightly pressing, got into his pyjamas and extinguished the lamp on the dressing-table. As he settled himself comfortably an air from the musical comedy they had seen that night started in the shallows of his mind. Pleased that he should remember it so well, he started humming it and immediately went wrong. Yet the thing went on singing itself accurately in the mind. Strange that was and significant.

His mother was still in his mind and yet she was not of it. She was dead; and she was the only one to whom he ever felt himself accountable. His renunciation of her influence liberated him. He did not feel lonely: he was elevated, excited. He was free.

That was why he had not told Elizabeth. Tenderness and all that was very good and fine; but if he could take his heart to task and argue with it he knew it must admit its joy at being free and untrammelled. Now there was no one to spy on him, no one to stand hooded and apart watching his thoughts and actions. He was alone. The trick of his mother's vision had been an evocation of his moral sense. He had worked intuitively upon his memories of her in the ordering of his life, and so practised became his inner eye that on any deviation, however slight, he saw his error torture the face of truth.

All was slumbrously serene. The Venetian blinds on the windows were open slightly, and regular slits of light from a street-lamp near by climbed his wall like a ladder, blue as moonlight. A coal in the dying fire stirred and sank into the ashes below. Far off in the city an engine screamed, and the echo sustained a picture of flurrying smoke over a deserted street. These were dear familiar things in the night's silence. The quick and the living were resting.

It was in the office that his new sense of liberty was most fully realized, and of the office Elizabeth knew only as much as he told her. His instinctive movement, for all their friendliness, was away from her and towards the men around him during the day. He was junior clerk on the staff of Johnston and Main, coalmasters and shippers, in Saint Vincent Street, appointed when he was barely twenty through the influence of Uncle James, and now after three years of service assisting at the invoice desk along with Clifford, his immediate senior, and the charge hand, Mr Speedie. In the affairs of the office he had been found a willing lad, obliging and trustworthy, and able to be left alone with work of some responsibility. But despite this aspect of him he escaped utter condemnation by the staff only because he was a son of the manse. Moral hypocrisy was expected of him, and in showing himself dourly ill-pleased when the boys were ribald, in his evidence of a moral obstinacy when jokes and innuendoes were flying about, he was easily classified by men used to card-indexes and dockets. The modern indictment of Puritanism was directed naturally against him by men of an honest depravity.

For long enough he had not known how to treat these

men. His experience was too slight for him to have tested his scruples. All about him were people living emancipated lives and making a show of it. They were emergents from respectability and Scottish Puritanism. They were 'Not Hypocrites', a term which described an active philosophy of modern life. By their honesty they were saving the community from complete corruption. At the same time they were able to indulge unashamedly in whatever graceful vice the hypocrite might keep hidden. And David, listening and watching, liked them. He turned away, but he was fascinated. They had their fling at Puritanism, they were cruel and exaggerated about the Church's failings, all with intent to wound him. It made no difference: he liked them through it all. But no warmth of heart could resist the chill that fell upon him when they were nasty. He blundered and was awkward then, his very hands and feet becoming clumsy.

He knew they drew a fine distinction between his moral reserve and natural instincts. When they were not purposefully bullying him with coarse talk, they might flatter him into thoughts of his popularity. He was included in most of the office schemes and intrigues, he had been to supper at Mr Speedie's, and on several occasions Bessie Fowlis had asked him to a party at her house. The only mark of inferiority he carried was this moral stinginess and cowardice, this unclarified desire to remain furtive and alone in certain things.

But now a springtime lightness was lifting his mind. A freshness was getting into his muscles and his bones. In a very short time, by simply refusing to feel, he would cease being awkward and clumsy. If this new freedom meant anything it surely meant an end to the men's despising. Already he had a suspicion that in avoiding their ways of living he had been missing something rather wonderful. Clifford, for instance, with whom he was most friendly, being at his elbow all day and coffeeing with him in the afternoons, what did he really think? It was almost impossible to tell; and yet Clifford was the real test. A word from him and the office was easy or difficult. Against his encroaches David had been most stubborn, for his worldliness had been consistently polished and unforced. Clifford could fascinate anyone by his bored accounts of orgies as being 'not too bad', he could repel suddenly, violently, by a story of callousness that was, somehow, like a revelation of smoky darkness within him. David's incredulity would take some shape which annoyed the easy Clifford. 'It's a game you're playing,' he might say: 'I know. You accuse me of being a hypocrite. But in saying you are as bad as that you are a hypocrite. I don't believe you're nearly as bad as you make out.' All of this would bring an oath from Clifford in the coinage of his complete debasement. At other times, when they were coffeeing in Haggart's in the afternoon, David might let him talk on unchecked, and Clifford, sensing perhaps in his companion's silence an inner audience at once credulous and shy, would recount his social conquests or adventures in a bored reluctant manner. The end generally came with an exclamation, 'But why do I tell you all this? Why do you want to listen?' or 'But you're the outside edge, you are! Are you jealous?' which restored each of them to his wonted plane.

David did not dream of telling Clifford that something had come over him or gone from him. So far all he wanted was but a tentative reaching out to examine. If he could not tell Elizabeth, far less was it possible to tell Clifford, who would have sneered the whole fineness of the thing away. But, just as with Elizabeth, he was revealing to Clifford's eyes something of the freshness and lightness of his new mental state, and day by day Clifford seemed more amiably disposed toward him.

One afternoon when they reached Haggart's, which was a small room above a tobacconist's shop in Gordon Street, they had Mr Razzle, the shipping manager, at their heels. This was Mr Razzle's 'howf' as much as theirs, and both parties rather resented the intrusion of the other. To the older man it was a strain on the discipline of the office to be continually coming up against the juniors in a coffeeroom; to the juniors his presence was a menace to their leisure. It was up to the boys to choose a new place, and Glasgow is rich in coffeerooms, but this Clifford refused to do. He looked at Mr Razzle's 'clock', as he not inappropriately called that gentleman's face, with extreme nonchalance, nodding, if he were recognized, in exact proportion to Mr Razzle's greeting, and then under his breath repeating his stale joke, 'There's Old Bill in a better 'ole.'

Mr Razzle was a man of middle age, bearing an air of prosperity which suggested Clifford's epigram. Without his bluff and swagger he would have been a comical figure with shaggy moustache, satanic eyebrows and puffed-out cheeks. His gush and rapid movements were a covering-up which distracted the eye from the crude framework of his face.

He watched the boys closely. Once or twice he had caught a glance his way and known that they were talking of him as they smoked cigarettes and sipped their coffee. At other times their indifference worried him. It was not right that his presence should not impinge itself to some extent upon their freedom. He would have expected a show of respect, even though they never looked his way. But they slouched; they lay back negligently on their chairs; they guffawed; they behaved without the remotest concern for the official eye. And, on this particular day when he had followed them so closely, they secured his favourite table near the window and called on Gracie to attend them in the most lordly manner.

Clifford, when he was satisfied he had all David's attention, peered over at Mr Razzle, his eyes narrowed to slits. Then sitting back he murmured mysteriously:

'Heard the news about Old Bill?'

'No.'

'He's after Bessie.'

'Bessie Fowlis! Surely not!'

'Fact.'

'I say, Clifford, how d'you know?'

'For certain. That's how I know. He's getting busy.'

It was the most casual thing in the world. One of a thousand observations that could be made on a man's natural behaviour. But the man whom David saw when he glanced over covertly was middle-aged, with a bushy moustache and a round bald spot on the top of his head. He had a sagging underlip and furtive, quick-moving blue eyes. The old instinct came over David.

'Beast!' he pouted.

Clifford clenched the stem of his pipe between his teeth viciously. He did not object to Razzle being called a beast; but this particular reference incriminated more than Razzle.

'Don't be soft,' he growled, turning his eyes away contemptuously.

Gracie the waitress came with their coffee and wrote out a check for sixpence. 'Thanks, Gracie,' Clifford smiled. 'Is that all you have for me today?'

'That's all.'

'Wouldn't like to write a wee love letter on the other side?'

'Get on with you now,' she laughed, and moved away.

But David was thinking over this matter of Bessie Fowlis. How did Clifford know? She was the telephone-operator and a very decent sort. When David had started work in the office she was the only one who had made any effort to put him at his ease. She sat all day with the telephone gear on her head attending to the plugs, and if she did chew gum interminably her excuse of keeping a clear whistle was more than adequate for David. To hear Clifford speak so coarsely about her pained him. But he dared not reveal any more of that to Clifford: he wanted to hear the story.

'Bessie Fowlis, eh?' he managed to leer. 'Who'd have thought it!'

'Oh, I dunno. I could have told you ages ago.'

'How did you get wind of it?'

'I went into the office one night for my golf-clubs. When I arrived I found Bessie sitting in her room reading. Then in bounces Razzle-dazzle, in a hell of a hurry. He didn't expect to find me, and the look on his face was enough. You should have seen Bessie's face, too! She was mad!'

Clifford smacked his lips appreciatively.

'And then?' asked David breathlessly.

'Oh, they made some show of it and I cleared out as soon as I could with my clubs. But I nearly laughed in old Razzle's face.'

David was profoundly stirred. The situation was too dramatic for him to join in Clifford's enjoyment. He looked at his friend as he might at some actor reminiscing off stage.

'And you really think they were there to meet each other?'

Clifford looked down his nose at David's shoes. 'Of course they were, you idiot.'

'Don't you think they might be serious? I mean—'

'You're an ass, Carruthers. Use your wits. A man like that, in a west-end flutter over himself, going with Bessie? Don't be soft.'

David looked over once more at Mr Razzle. Was it possible that such a man, who in his gushing manner asserted and even imposed on others the ordinary conventions of good behaviour, could actually make an appointment with Bessie Fowlis? It seemed queer. And possibly he would make his advances with such a gusto and heartiness of inanity that Bessie would be completely taken in.

'I can hardly believe it,' David sighed.

'What's in it, anyway?' Clifford grunted. 'Sure that sort of thing's going on all over the town. Nothing in it. Come on: it's your turn to pay.'

David lifted the check Gracie had left on their table and they went downstairs.

'Got any money to spare?' Clifford asked easily when they were in the street.

'A few bob, I think.'

'Could you lend me ten till Friday?'

'Sure.'

As Clifford accepted the money he seemed to be thinking of something quite different. At last he said:

'Thanks. Doing anything tonight?'

'No.'

'Well, let's have a night up town. That's what I wanted the money for, really; I feel in the mood.'

David hesitated, but only for a second, and then in a manner almost as casual as Clifford's he agreed.

'Right you are. Where shall I see you?'

'Wellington Street car stop and sharp at seven-thirty.' Clifford laughed. 'I'll make a man of you in a single night.'

David found him at the appointed time standing on the doorstep of the La Scala Cinema surveying the drifting crowds on the pavement. 'Well,' Clifford began, 'what would you like to do? And remember—tonight's on me.'

'Oh, rubbish, Clifford,' David protested. He jingled his coins in his trouser pocket. 'I'll go my whack.'

'No.' Clifford was quite determined. 'It's on me. I've got some more cash unexpectedly. Anyway, I asked you out.'

That settled, he turned again to survey the crowds. He was dressed in a light raincoat, bowler hat and spats, and he carried white gloves. He seemed unlike himself to David, who had never seen him 'up town' before. This haughty sociability was also something new.

'I tell you what,' he said. 'Let's have a quick one round the corner.'

They slipped into the traffic for a few seconds and passed into Wellington Street, where they made for a quiet bar Clifford knew.

'What'll you have?'

David had never been in such a place before. It was a single apartment with a short broad counter lined with glass slabs under which were paper doilies of various patterns. Bottles of all sizes and colours were ranged on broad shelves backed by flashing mirrors, and a burnished cash-register attached to the counter added to the blaze of reflection and dazzle in which the electric light was dissipated. The place was empty save for the barmaid, who was sitting at an open fire by the door reading a cheap magazine.

'Ginger beer, I think,' murmured David, as though afraid the barmaid might hear.

'A baby B and a ginger ale, please,'

Clifford was playing the perfect gentleman. He produced some Turkish cigarettes and they lit up. The barmaid laid two glasses before them, took the money and resumed her seat at the fire. David was watching Clifford and repeating his every move. The natural thing to expect now was that they got ahead with the drinks. But Clifford was in no hurry. You don't drink beer immediately it is laid before you. You light a cigarette and look round, torturing yourself in a final moment of expectancy, when the thing is there before you and nothing short of an earthquake or a heart-seizure can separate you. It is a moment of ecstasy created by the twin sensations of self-gratification and self-thwarting. In such a moment you indulge yourself and yet exercise a full self-discipline.

'This is not a pub, David,' Clifford explained leisurely, and glanced about him. 'This is a bar. There's a queer difference, really. A pub's a—a pub. There's nothing like it. We'll go to one later and you'll see for yourself.'

This was a new Clifford. He still had his superior air—that was inevitable as the result of his greater experience and age; but his voice had lost its drawl of boredom and had a dash of kindliness in it. He treated David with a courtesy that was scrupulous and polished.

'Well,' he sighed, and stretched a lazy hand toward the beer, 'here's to luck to you.' Raising it to his lips he drained the glass at a single tilt, his eyes turning upwards sepulchrally. He sighed again as he laid down a frothy glass and his lips twisted in an expression of anguish as though he had swallowed a gallon of gall. 'That was good,' he murmured.

David was finding the ginger bitter and gaseous. A mouthful of it filled him and he had to wait while it abated. Clifford, noting his slowness, decided he had time for another.

'Same again for me, Bella, please.'

He actually knew the girl's name! And yet they had not as much as acknowledged each other at the beginning!

David held off his ginger ale until Clifford was served, and then he made a gallant effort and kept on drinking, drinking, although the rotten stuff seemed to be gurgling around his tonsils and refusing to flow down. When he was finished two empty glasses reposed before Clifford.

'Ready?'

David nodded and hiccoughed.

'Don't know how you can drink that stuff,' Clifford commented as he led the way.

It was dusk now and the city lights were full ablaze. Sauchiehall Street lay like a golden stream through a dark forest.

'What will we do now?' asked David.

Clifford was eyeing a couple of women who were sauntering up Wellington Street. 'Eh?' he exclaimed. 'Yes. Well, let's go to a pub. I'd like to show you a pub.'

Although he seemed to see something interesting in every woman his eyes encountered, Clifford made no remark. David felt rather disappointed. Going from a bar to a pub was poor enough fun. But the pubs shut at nine o'clock, and perhaps it was of this that Clifford was thinking. The women, and one of those daring exploits of which Clifford was always speaking at coffee-time, would come afterwards.

In a few minutes David found himself in a crowded public house. As the swing doors banged back behind him he had a shivering sensation in his spine, for he feared that some eye had observed him and was now staring in surprise at the place he had entered. A yellow glare, in which the hyacinth-coloured smoke from pipes and cigarettes floated languidly, brought water to his eyes, and the steady hum of voices jarred his mind confusingly. He heard Clifford's voice repeat the casual question, 'What's yours?' and it sounded like someone roaring instructions in a storm.

'Ginger ale,' he replied in a loud, clear voice.

A sandy-haired man, looking as bored as Clifford when Clifford was on duty, and wearing a soiled apron over his waistcoat, heard Clifford's request for a baby B and ginger ale without paying the least attention. David was on the point of suggesting that they should try another part of the counter when the man appeared and with a dexterous move planted two glasses before them. 'Eight-a-half-off-two,' he yelled into David's face, and wheeling round disappeared with Clifford's two shillings.

A man standing beside David was muttering to himself as he gazed into a deep brown liquid on the counter. He was talking to someone in his thoughts. Suddenly he would revive, incline to take a sip and instead spit lustily on the sawdusted groove provided for the purpose at his feet.

'Well,' sighed Clifford as his fingers embraced his glass, 'here's to luck to you,' and over went the third baby B. David found his ginger ale flat and was grateful for it. He was not very long after Clifford in laying down an empty glass.

Clifford's lips had resumed their normal lines. Evidently the expression of acute distaste after beer was a form of

ritual, just as that mumbled 'here's to luck to you' was a
form of grace before meals.

'Could you have another?'

David's face looked serious. But, gallant still, he nodded
assent and said:

'Won't you let me—?'

'This is on me.' Clifford caught the eye of the sandy-haired
barman. 'A baby B and a ginger ale, please, Archie.'

David was interrupted in his wonder at this by a disturb-
ance behind. The thoughtful fellow at his elbow was looking
round; a fat barman with a gold watch-chain over the
front of his white apron was watching critically. Suddenly
there was a most horrible retching. David glanced round
nervously and saw a man in working clothes empty a
deranged stomach on the sawdust. David grasped the edge
of the counter.

'Eight-a-half-off-one,' came a yell at his ear, and Clifford
pushed the ginger ale toward him.

He was desperate for some distraction, and thinking that
it was only right to talk about workmen in a pub, he began
in an argumentative tone:

'Do you think the miners are underpaid, Clifford?'

'Everyone is underpaid,' Clifford replied. 'Small wages
are a curse. They lead to all sorts of vices—gambling, drinking, stealing and what not.'

'How does that come about?'

'Why shouldn't it?'

'If people haven't money to spend, I mean.'

'Statistics, my lad. Statistics.'

'I can understand in a way, you know,' David reflected.

'Yes, small wages are a curse. But,' with a glance behind
him, Clifford went on languidly, 'these miners are a bloody
nuisance.' A young boy in a big barman's apron was now
shovelling and re-sawdusting. 'They can't even carry their
liquor.'

Clifford seemed to be carrying his well. It was not the

quantity that surprised David—he himself had consumed
rather more in actual quantity—though that did seem excess-
ively large; it was the alcohol contained in Clifford's stuff.
Was all the temperance talk about beer being intoxicating
untrue? His eyes searched Clifford's face, but could discover no trace of loosening forces in that serene countenance.

Having finished their drinks the question arose, 'What
will we do now?'

'We'll wander down town, I think,' said Clifford. 'Perhaps we'll drop in at the Central and see about a drink
there.'

It was a relief not to be making a beeline for a pub.
They crossed into Renfield Street, which was alive with
electrical advertisements, and edged their way through the
crowds. Once Clifford drew up and looked behind, his eyes
narrowed keenly. 'What is it?' David asked hopefully. He
got the direction of Clifford's gaze and saw two young
women glancing back.

'Eh, what?' exclaimed Clifford, coming back to realities.
'Sorry, David, old fellow. Were you saying something?'

David was too disappointed to reply. He shook his head
and they resumed their walk.

Out of the stream of people on the pavement came a
shout: 'Clifford! Hullo there!' Two young fellows without overcoats, in immaculate suits with handkerchiefs and
ties to match, gushed at Clifford's elbows.

'Where are you going, old chap?' they stormed him.

'Hullo, Skinner, 'lo, Donaldson. Oh, just knocking
about. Yes, Skinny, my lad, you fair did it on Saturday.
Jolly fine. I say, this is a friend of mine, Carruthers.'

David had always thought Rugby a bore: but here were
celebrities. He had seen this fellow Skinner in the papers
and in the newsreels. David shook hands as though self-
abnegation were a sacrament. But the Rugby giants were
charitable fellows, and they hailed David as one of the hot
dogs of their own kind.

'Let's have a drink somewhere,' said Skinner.

'Where?'

'Any old place. Where were you going?'

A burst of laughter.

'Thought of dropping in at the Central,' said Clifford meekly.

'The Central will be pleased!'

'Jolly decent of you, you know!'

They laughed and gurgled. For a few minutes Clifford forgot his self-imposed task as host to David, but as soon as he recovered himself his impeccable manner returned. His hand held David's elbow lightly as they all trooped into the lounge of the hotel.

Skinner became involved with the waiter, but Clifford pushed him aside.

'This is on me. What are you having?'

'Beer, I think,' said Donaldson.

'Beer for me,' said Skinner.

'Three beers and a ginger ale,' said Clifford.

Skinner gurgled anew. 'Ginger ale! You're a great lad, Cliffy. Who's taking that gargle?'

'My friend's had too much to drink already tonight,' Clifford replied gallantly. 'I refuse to allow him anymore booze.'

'Snakes!' exclaimed Donaldson, turning to David. 'Do you stand for that?'

'I think he's right,' David managed to say. 'Yes, really,' as Skinner made to recall the waiter, 'I'd prefer ginger this time.'

Skinner shrugged his shoulders and sat down heavily in a chair. 'Right y'are.'

'Gracious!' David heard a light voice exclaim somewhere near, and then there was a titter. Skinner looked past David, and his face gradually became placid until all that was left of his merriment was a twinkle in his clear blue eyes now engaging the attention of a group of girls at the next table.

Thereafter events developed quickly and David found himself being ushered into the company of the girls with elaborate courtesy by Skinner, who was convinced he was drunk. The mistake which Clifford, either artfully or thoughtlessly, had engineered, was very fortunate; for every clumsy action or word his embarrassment caused would now naturally be regarded in a tolerant light. He succumbed to the easy method of appearing to be drunk in order to save himself from some vague disgrace he feared if his ordinary sober self were judged by these quick-witted youths and self-assured young women.

He got seated beside a girl to whom he was formally introduced by Clifford after Clifford had inquired her name. With mock gravity Clifford continued this performance with each member of the company until the circle was complete. David was paired off with a Miss Ryan.

'The nights are closing in quickly now, aren't they?' he ventured to her when the others were engaged among themselves.

'Oh yes.'

'Do you work in town?'

'No. I stay at home and help Mamma.' The girl whispered this theatrically as though her mother might be within reach. Then she giggled and it was David's turn, in his sudden confusion, to murmur 'Oh yes.' He glanced over at Clifford nervously. The girl had realized he was a fool pretty quickly. Blessedly, however, Clifford had not observed.

It had been by the merest chance that Skinner had set him down beside this girl who was, at a glance, the most attractive of the bunch, and it was noticeable how this fortunate chance affected the attitude of the men towards him. It was an additional burden upon his confidence, however, and he cursed inwardly with disappointment that poor old Clifford had not got the pretty girl instead.

He need have had no regrets on that score. When they all rose to depart there was some necessary sidestepping for hats and coats, and as they assembled again it so happened that Clifford and Miss Ryan were together and David was companioned by a Miss Low.

'The nights are drawing in quickly nowadays, aren't they?' he risked once more.

'Yes, they are,' the girl replied. She was a nice plain-spoken person, different from Miss Ryan.

They marched down the wide deep-carpeted stairs. 'Do you work in town?'

'Yes—well, nearly; in Maryhill.'

'I see.'

A halt was called beyond the hotel door in the station proper. David watched Clifford write something in his diary with Miss Ryan craning her neck at his shoulder.

'Right-o,' Clifford was saying. 'I'll write and let you know.'

There was a general parting. Miss Low and Miss Ryan were going home; Miss Smith and Miss Crawford were waiting with Skinner and Donaldson. Suddenly David had his arm pulled savagely and Clifford's face swam before him.

'Do you see the time, David?'

It was 8.54.

'The Rat-pit, quick! Put your skates on.'

Clifford led the way to the Rat-pit, a small bar in the station beside the carriage-way and the telephone kiosks. It was smaller than the one in Wellington Street, and in spite of its open entrance to the dusty station it was neat and cosy.

The boys hurried to the counter.

'A baby B and a ginger ale, please,' said Clifford breathlessly.

But in spite of the scanty minutes remaining Clifford would not treat his beer with disrespectful haste. He opened himself to an awareness of these minutes, demanding that they should be lived intensely, and the added dignity of his pipe, which he was now smoking, gave this final drink of the evening its due solemnity. David gallantly depended on the last reserves of his strength; he felt beneath him the loose, wobbling substance of hysteria; he dared not laugh lest he should be gassed, dared not cough lest he should vomit. One thing remained as he hung suspended in time and space; that he should quench an alleged thirst with this last long ginger ale. Its amber had no heart of light for him, no sparkle, no effervescence, no winking bubbles. It was solid liquid, heavy as lead: solid prickly lead that poured as liquid down his cleansed and experienced throat. He knew the tricks to combat ginger ale by this time; the threatening hiccough that could be baffled by a sudden holding-in of the breath; the boke that could be disguised as a clearing of the throat; the fizzing in the nose that could be minimized by a discreet sniff. This was an age of record-breaking. Surely he had added, unknown and inglorious as it must remain, one more achievement to the honour of his day!

It was finished, and the hands of the clock pointed starkly to a minute past nine. Gently he turned to Clifford.

'What will we do now?'

The answer was less incisive than formerly; but, determined to be cheerful, even though he were now on the outer rim of darkness, Clifford replied airily:

'Let's wander up town. We'll go into a café, maybe, and see what's doing. The girls should be there by this time.'

They climbed the steps out of the bar and strolled alongside the empty telephone boxes. David was on the point of saying something about the early closing hours, on which he was but poorly informed, when, without warning, a gaseous tumult arose within him. His little tricks were then as feeble as gauze against a poison-gas attack. His nose tingled as though a thistle had been pulled through it; he sneezed violently, hiccoughed, and then, standing still, gave utterance to a prolonged thunderous rift which brought an abiding look of admiration into Clifford's eyes. It was so absurdly vulgar as to be a high-class social grace. Clifford leaned against a kiosk and roared.

'That's the stuff,' he gurgled; 'get rid of it somehow. Gee, you've enough gas in you to light the city.'

'I say, Clifford, I'm so sorry. I'm full of wind, right enough.'

'Eh, what, you are! But we'd better get on. If you behave like that here we'll have a crowd round us.'

Though he did not enlarge on it, David was immensely relieved. But it was only for the time being. As they were walking up Hope Street the rumblings started once more and vapours invaded his eyes. He swayed slightly.

As he steadied himself an awful thought occurred to him. Perhaps he was drunk. What did the word *ale* mean anyway? Perhaps everything that was sold in a pub or bar was intoxicating. That might be one of the stipulations of the trade. His brow was damp with perspiration. Clutching at Clifford's arm in a timid appealing manner, he stammered:

'Say, Clifford, is ginger ale intoxicating?'

'No, you fathead,' laughed Clifford, forgetting his duty as host for the moment. 'Ginger ale, be God!' he muttered to himself. 'How? Do you feel tight?'

'I—I wondered.'

'It's wind that's the matter with you. A cup of tea'll set you right.'

From Hope Street they found their way to a popular house where tearooms and a dance hall were associated with a cinema, each place giving access to the others. They sought a retiring room where they washed and refreshed themselves, Clifford combing his dark sleek hair straight back from his unruffled brows and David rubbing his face vigorously with his handkerchief. The tearoom was loud with the noise of dance music and the clatter of china. A faint thread of human voices sounded through the din, faint as the bluey smoke from cigarettes threading the golden glow from smothered lamps in alabaster bowls and baskets of silk. Clifford and David stood awhile on the fringe of affairs, accustoming their eyes to the atmosphere, and ultimately a waitress, sizing them up, pointed to a table at which there were two vacant chairs. Clifford shook his head and refused the prompting.

'We're looking for someone,' he lied blandly.

Giving an appearance of truth to this, David exclaimed, 'There's Bessie Fowlis!'

Clifford looked over.

'And she's with a pal.' His eyes glinted. 'Well, what about it?' he asked, turning round. 'Will we? I'll take Bessie, and you can have her friend. But if we see the friend's no good we'll sheer off. See? You give me the wire.'

David followed Clifford. It seemed that everyone in that place must envy him his graceful easygoing companion.

'Clifford!' exclaimed Bessie as they approached, '—and David! My lad, are you leading this youth astray?'

'You will have your little joke, Bessie,' murmured Clifford, humbly surveying David.

'Come and sit down,' Bessie invited them in the friendliest tones. 'This is my friend, Jessie Adair.'

Soon they had Jessie smiling happily. They told her of the relative positions on the staff of Messrs Johnston and Main, and gave her well-worn stories of Mr Speedie and others. Talk then turned to cinema stars and to those appearing in the film which the girls had just seen in the picture house next door. Bessie was suave and benevolent. Jessie, dressed in a green knitted costume and green leather hat, fawn stockings and green shoes, possessed an agreeable smile which made amends for a too large mouth. She was docile as a well-nourished cat.

David had started off by telling her that the nights were drawing in quickly nowadays and that winter would soon be upon them, both of which reminders seemed to gratify her. 'I hate the summer in town,' she said. 'It's so dusty and cold and yet you've to wear summer clothes; and the daylight is so long you simply can't do anything at night.'

'Awful bore.'

Thereafter they made quick progress. He glanced brightly at Clifford, doing his utmost to give him 'the wire'. But Clifford was strange. He seemed unimpressed by this green-clad Jessie and made signs that he was going to rescue David. He was being prompted by that queer sense of loyalty to a pal which denies the claims of any girl not immediately attractive to himself. David, perceiving this, exaggerated his winks and appreciative nods until at last Clifford, against his better judgment, had to acknowledge the signals and set about arranging matters.

They parted outside the café, Clifford taking Bessie south and David going with Jessie. They took the car to Partickhill, and by the time they reached her street, a narrow tenemented aisle called Black Street, they regarded themselves as old friends.

'It's early yet,' said David boldly.

'Fairly,' she agreed.

'Won't you show me the back?'

By this he meant the back stair of the close which led to the bleaching greens and the middens. In most tenements the back yard is a black aperture neglected at night by all save such young people returning from the city or a cinema. Jessie, laughing roguishly, led the way, guiding him by the hand.

She took him down some steps into a black hollow in which they were utterly hidden from each other. But she knew the place well, and backed up against a padlocked cellar. The air was chill, with a subterranean smell of damp and rubbish.

They did not speak. Possibly she wished to avoid any risk of being found there. And, in any case, they need not go to such a place for conversation. The girl frankly accepted their reason for being there and in her experience was eager for it. So soon, then, as she was comfortably settled against the cellar door, which she knew to be smooth and comparatively clean, she threw her arms round David's neck and drew him to her. Her head was lowered to his shoulder, but somehow in that first sightless embrace it was their lips which met, and it was she, in her expectancy of passion, who introduced it at once.

She did not guess that this youth was having his first taste of lip-salve and that hers were the first girlish arms to close round him. He was a boy with a boy's attractions for her developing womanhood and she presumed in him an intention as frank as her own. This was to disturb emotional reserves, to perplex and torture each other to the very brink of the final denial and then to make their pain a link of sympathy between them. But David, guarded and restricted by his awakened sense of wonder, was too flattered to be dangerous, too excited to be physically distressed. The glory of this occasion, which made him an equal adventurer with Clifford, created the glow she felt to be tenderness and passion. His endurance pleased her.

But during the long tram journey to the other side of Glasgow and the walk up Cornfoot Avenue in the uneasy suburban quiet before midnight the glow of wonder in his mind was dissipated. He was restored to the level of his former ignorance, just as now he was returning to the house of his childhood. His body was fouled and soured by ginger ale and lip-salve and the smell of face-cream and scent. The exercise of walking restarted the disorders of his stomach, which was still gaseous and unquiet. He resented the burning sensation in his throat and chest, he was maddened by the irrepressible rifting. To relieve himself of the smell of face-cream he blew his nose violently, and to rid himself of the taste of lip-salve he washed his lips with his handkerchief wetted by his tongue. But it was no use. This night life of Clifford's had poisoned him with its tastes and smells. It had overtaxed his stomach with its ale and tea.

The sense of guilt and physical uncleanness depressed him further when he entered his bedroom. Everything he touched, the cool chaste sheets of his single bed, the pyjama-case, the cold-water jug, contrasted vividly with the depravity of the night's behaviour. Elizabeth had arranged these things with her usual care for his comfort, moving about the room and wondering why he was so late.

He got into bed and lay hugging the hot-water bottle. Such a stupid inane way of spending a night that had been. Its chief fun had consisted in pretending to enjoy it.

Was there ever anything more shallow than that?

He would go out with Clifford no more.

But in the morning all seemed different. Clifford glanced brightly at him as soon as he entered the office, and when they got settled at the desk together he grinned in the friendliest fashion. It was not an evil grin. It had not the guile or cruelty Clifford's expression often had. Rather it was bright and friendly, friendly in a new winning way. David on a sudden upwelling of gratitude realized he could not let Clifford down when he looked so decent. So he grinned back knowingly. Then he heard Clifford's theatrical aside to Mr Speedie. 'David's been pulling our legs: he's really a hell of a fellow.'

'Indeed!' came Mr Speedie's stage whisper.

'Was up town with him last night,' Clifford went on, now in his normal tone, 'and he disappeared with a woman.'

'She wasn't a woman, Clifford,' David remonstrated; 'she's just a kid.'

'I'll bet you've put a date on with her, anyway!'

'But, do you know who he went away with?' David turned animatedly to Mr Speedie. 'Bessie Fowlis!'

'Huh!' Nothing could surprise Mr Speedie. 'You'd better watch Razzle-dazzle doesn't get to know.'

The boys glanced at each other.

'I merely took her away from her friend so that David could have a clear field.' And again Clifford grinned.

It was all very nice, this quiet banter. It was pally and intimate. The absence of the old slighting attitude was something positive which warmed David to the men. They were chaffing him, but now it was on their own ground, almost as they might expect to be chaffed themselves, and Clifford had a glimmer of respect in his eyes which made all the difference in the world.

During the forenoon, however, the word was passed round the office that David had been up town with Clifford, and the situation was subtly changed. Winston Bruce and Mr Walls, the shipping clerks who assisted Mr Razzle, sauntered over to the desk and with too bold an innocence wanted to know the story of David's girl. Miss Gordon, the typist, had it from Bessie that David's lounge behaviour was exquisite; that it was something to be coveted by men and guarded against by women. There came a suggestion of mockery in everything that was said, and David in his responses had to battle against this hidden menace as well as skirmish pleasantly upon the surface of the banter. If they were mocking him he was lost. If they mocked him it was because he had been tricked out of his superiority, exposed and condemned.

When they were alone in Haggart's he made his appeal to Clifford.

'Look here, I wish you hadn't told everyone about last night. I've a rotten feeling that they're laughing at me.'

'Not a bit of it,' Clifford assured him. Clifford was back to his usual bored attitude but prepared to be magnanimous.

'You'll have to follow it up, of course,' he said. 'Did you really arrange to see her again?'

David admitted that he had not.

'You should have done that!' Clifford spoke as a senior would upon some fault in office routine.

'I should have asked her, I suppose; to a theatre or something, eh?'

'Well,' Clifford drawled, 'you should have asked her out. Theatre's expensive. But have it your own way. You'll learn by and by to get all you want and never see a theatre.'

It was lackadaisically said, yet it was overpowering. Never had David heard anything with so much certainty of experience and understanding behind it. Had it been spoken jokingly or with a lewd jeer he would have taken it as he had taken so much else of a questionable nature today. But it was meant as a serious expression of faith in which Clifford felt his right to a superiority that must needs be one of boredom, the boredom of extreme familiarity. Not to contest it meant for David a tacit renunciation of all decency. The moment held him imperilled before a tide of darkness that would quench the springtime lightness in his heart and drown for ever the picture of his mother in the back regions of his mind.

Yet he did not contest it, and in the days which immediately followed he was to remember his silence as a conquest over his besetting impetuosity. He had been on the point of a reckless speech, such a speech as on other occasions he had ventured, an exclamation, 'Oh, Clifford, that sounds terribly depraved!' or, more didactic, an appeal to Clifford's better nature with, 'But you can't mean that. You make yourself much worse than you are when you say that; therefore you're a hypocrite because you're a snob.' The urge was acute, but he mastered it. He knew what would have happened had he spoken. Clifford would have scorned him and he would have been miserable. An awkwardness would have come into his joints as though he had been devitalized by some drug. Rather than brave all that once again and lose what he had gained last night, he let the wave of darkness flow over him. His eyelids fluttered as though performing a nod of understanding and then he looked away.

Clifford lay back in his chair, contented enough for all the minute signs of boredom. There was a careless air about him and yet he was precise in every movement and precise in his attire, which gave a first impression of carelessness. The collar of his waterproof was curled against his neck as it had been when he was out in the smirr of the wintry afternoon. The coat was loose, showing a dark tweed suit beneath, and on the cuff of one sleeve a button dangled on its last thread. That untidy button on a damp soiled waterproof over an expensive suit was just right. It was all the rage in Glasgow to have a waterproof of this sort, like an overall, for the business of disregarding Glasgow's murky weather. The button quivered and flashed as his hand trifled with the pipe which he was treating with a delicate finesse. Clifford could no more have clutched that pipe clumsily than he could have bruised the arm of a woman. Nor did he envelop his head in smoke from extravagant blowing and puffing. His lips were faintly moist and but touched the shining vulcanite, whereat there was a dainty curl of smoke from the bowl; he ran the stem slowly along his lips and a tiny thread of smoke followed; he had the pipe poised under his mouth and slowly his head drooped until his lips were level again. The art of smoking a pipe gracefully was more satisfying than the fragrance of the choicest mixture.

'Yes,' he sighed, as though he had finally weighed up the situation. 'You'd better get her address from Bessie or her phone number and fix it up.'

No more was said: they finished their coffee and went back to the office.

Elizabeth had not arrived when he reached home in the evening; but Maisie, whose night out it was, had left the table at the ivy window set for tea, and a fire was still lively on the hearth. He had not been in this room for over twenty-four hours, and when he looked round now he found it, safe from the cold and the wind, in a beneficent calm. Yet with its choice details made up of memoried things it was some-how strangely aloof. Now that he had this letter to write tonight, now that his mind was excited over new worldly things, it seemed rapt and apart in its own domestic dream.

What was there to do meanwhile? He could not sit down at once and rush off the letter. Elizabeth was liable to come in at any minute and interrupt. There should be other things to do. In the old days—yesterday, a month or a year ago—he had had no need to put the question to himself. There was work about the house which, being their own property, required attention here and there; there was work waiting him in the tool-house. And there were books and magazines to read, the piano, the gramophone. Tonight every one of these was as a beckoning hand he brushed aside with loathing. There was only one thing to do, the letter to Jessie; and until it was written nothing could interest him, while after it was posted, he foresaw, nothing would matter until he met her.

He was going to do as Clifford advised. He might change his mood a hundred times, but he would write that letter and get Jessie to meet him again. Even in the train coming home he had had this resolve strengthened. In the compartment with him were fellows of his own age or slightly older, and as he looked at them he had been convinced, working intuitively upon their broad likeness to Clifford in attitude and movement, that they would do the same. And there was Jessie herself. He had not told Clifford exactly what had happened. But Clifford had presumed correctly, and what had happened seemed sure enough. The whole thing seemed to fit together like the divided parts of a riddle on which he had been gazing unintelligently for years.

When he had wandered aimlessly from the big room to the kitchen and upstairs to his own room, he entered the dining-room for the electric kettle, which he plugged. Then he stood motionless, his fingers on the side, to marvel anew at the swiftly dawning heat. The room was cold and silent. It was not such a pleasant room as the other. But it contained one thing which all the others lacked, and the presence of this had always given the room an importance and solemnity. Opposite him where he now stood, and slightly above the level of his eyes, was his mother's portrait. Her presence amid the shadows of the gilt frame and the magic of the toy at his hand were as an agitation at the heart of the room's silence.

Although he knew that portrait better than anything else in the house, he felt a shock as of a new discovery when he saw that the eyes were not looking at him. He left the kettle and moved, speculatively, the full extent of her gaze; but the eyes evaded him. It was a trick, of course; a subtle touch of paint had diffused her gaze so that she looked everywhere and nowhere. But it was such a trick as now, in the mood of this hour, was of peculiar significance. She would never look on him again. She knew nothing. And it was no use thinking that this was a brutal aggressive thought to have in this room. No impulsive remark to Clifford could be more importunate, maybe; but it was true. She knew nothing. Father knew nothing. Elizabeth need know nothing. He was free. 'It was only a superstitious idea I had,' he thought. As the words sounded in his brain and he faced the portrait squarely, the timid little person seemed to cringe within the frame. She cringed as from an assault.

But that was a trick of his own mind. He was remonstrating with himself for his relief at her nothingness, for over her nothingness something evil was triumphing. Or was it only different customs, different views, different faith? He remembered the day after the funeral when, knowing that he was bound to smile some time, he had gone to this portrait and bravely smiled up to her. How vivid she had seemed then! Now, after long years, history was repeating itself. He was looking up at the portrait admitting her nothingness.

When Elizabeth arrived he had the tea ready. She brought home a caseful of linen and made her usual announcement that she'd need to work all evening. He was going out for a little, he said.

'Going out again?'

He need go only the length of the letterbox at Queen's Park; but he could not tell her of a letter.

'Yes.'

She was thinking of last night and of how late he had been.

'What happened last night?'

'I was at a party with Clifford.'

This news visibly disappointed her. She had been thinking differently. Her sudden drop of interest, however, David attributed to Clifford's name. He did not mention Clifford oftener than was needful. Once, at the office door, Clifford and she had met; but he had hurried her away. His action had been instinctive, to protect her from Clifford's assessing eyes and subsequent shrewd reflection. Thereafter, though she had seen him only for a moment, Clifford's name had to be protected from her, for even his name, it seemed, could suffer injury by the slight sniff it summoned or the direct wondering gaze she gave him at its sound. What on earth, her eyes asked, could he see in such a person?

Tonight, however, Clifford's name was an evocation of his mood. He was prepared to share the sniff with Clifford.

'A party? In Clifford's house?'

'No: one of his friends.'

'Enjoy it?'

'Oh yes, well enough.'

'Somehow I don't fancy a party with Clifford at it.'

She looked over brightly, her lips parting vivaciously, as though inevitably they should enjoy this sneer together. She waited on his responding smile and nod which came; but his eyes were not frank. Her smile slowly died away.

Realizing that he had not concealed his feelings, he sought immediately to confuse her impression.

'We're not so very unlike those people ourselves,' he remarked casually.

'The people at the party? What do you mean?'

'They are so entirely material. If father were here he'd say that all their interests were "worldly". And so are ours nowadays. All your interests are secular. So are mine.'

The vivacity had come back to her face. 'But, David, we had so much of—of that: the other thing, I mean.'

'Yes, I know; and so we turned our backs on the whole thing. We chased the congregation crowd from here and so on, as though making a clearance. It was a dead set against the Church, really.'

'Oh, I was fed up,' Elizabeth sighed.

'So was I. But it meant a definite renouncement, don't you see? We did it for peace and quietness, yet we didn't know what we did. It was a renouncement of the Church as much as of the congregation.'

'It wasn't much of a renunciation,' Elizabeth grumbled. 'You know what the Church meant to father. He was like a commercial traveller with patented beliefs he'd sell at a price. We were "in the know".'

'Yes,' David persisted, and now he was pursuing an argument with himself; 'but those people I saw last night are something less than merely churchless, and yet we're like them. They go farther than we do, of course. They've an idea that the whole system of moral responsibility and decency is controlled by a religion or a church. So, if you don't go to church you don't respond to or recognize the system.'

Elizabeth smiled. 'Were they as rum as that?'

'No, but seriously, Betty, they don't regard an attention to morals or—or religion as good form.'

'Not the done thing?'

'Not the done thing!'

He echoed her little phrase to escape the embarrassment it might bring him. She was being facetious—and simply because she was not interested. She had shown no thought for his distinction between churchgoing and moral responsibility because the basis of her life was moral. It had happened that way and she recognized no other. Physical cleanliness and orderliness were to her taste. She shrank from the idea of Clifford as from those elementary substances children learn to leave alone.

Yet the way she turned away now, the lift of her chin, the inwardness of her eyes' expression, made him suddenly uneasy. He rose from the table to reach for cigarettes on the mantelpiece and with his back to her asked:

'Do you think Calvinism is dead?'

'I don't know. Do you?'

'I think it served its purpose. But if we don't watch we may deserve another scourge like it.'

She had been pulling the dishes together for the kitchen. Pausing with them now in her hands, as she faced the door, she remarked airily, 'Well, I don't think Clifford and parties are good for you. They make you doleful.'

He heard her pass through the hall a minute or two afterwards, and later her sewing machine was purring in another room. It set up a thin reverberation throughout the house, like the faint rhythmic motion of a ship's engines felt on deck.

She was off to her work, completely deceived. Deceived into a bright airy contentment, thinking no doubt on how simple and safe he was. In her brightness and airiness, indeed, there was the suggestion of a superior being who knew of his essential decency better than he did himself. She was assured in her complacency, just as Clifford was. But she believed in her brother's goodness and Clifford in the world's ill.

By her he was flattered and encouraged, by Clifford he was mystified and tormented.

When he caught sight of Jessie approaching the theatre door

on the appointed night he forced his way toward her almost roughly through the small groups of people standing about. She had a fur wrap round her and below it a silk gown of palest green. He had not dreamed that she would look so well as this.

She was hatless and her waved hair flowed back into the collar of her fur, a lighter tone of the same soft brown. It was silken soft, with the delicately curved lines of a comb's narrow teeth still undisturbed amid it. For the first time he noticed how she held her head slightly tilted to one side, like a bird, giving an impression of fragility and gentleness. He had never seen this in anyone else, and it was to become, when they were still friendlier, an aspect of her to which his mind resorted in moments of tenderness and desire. He led her to the cloakroom and through perplexing corridors to the stalls, feeling a little flustered as though she were a romping child at his side. But when they were settled in their seats his mind quietened down and became a reflecting pool.

This was how she found it. In everything he said she was mirrored. She had been looking forward to this evening, had phoned and written him about it and got a second and a friendlier letter only that morning. Both of them had betrayed an eagerness that was like a filling-up of expectancy and which now overflowed upon them. She remembered their previous meeting and the spirit of frankness which had prevailed then made her confident now. She jumbled her sentences in her excitement, certainly, with such words as 'But you'll think I'm daft,' or 'I suppose I'm crazy'; but what she had to say about her pleasure in coming to meet him rejoiced his heart. He whispered back as much and then, their shoulders touching in those happily arranged stalls, they looked into each other's eyes and smiled. The excitement of the musical comedy did not sustain their interest. Probably the colour and racing moments of good dancing quickened their senses to a pitch where they wanted to ignore everything and turn in upon themselves. They wearied for the intervals when they might talk with no restraint.

'I seem to have known you for ages,' she said when at last they were seated with tea in the lounge.

'Funny how that happens with some people,' he replied; 'I suppose we're like each other in some way.'

'Or, say, we like each other?'

'That's it,' he said simply. He wondered how Clifford would have taken this. By what easy turn, what graceful move would he have made use of it to advance his plan? But Clifford would have been untroubled by a secretive self-stirring within him: unaffected, save in one way, by the girl's fragile beauty and frank and likeable manner. There were things about people that Clifford simply didn't notice. Or perhaps he was blind and couldn't notice them. David's lips were dry; there was an unusual throbbing at his throat. Why should he continue to notice more than Clifford? There would be an hour after the theatre when a chance would be offered him, a certain positive chance. Looking ahead, it might be all Clifford's way despite the slight embarrassment her beauty caused him now.

'Do you come to the theatre often?' he asked.

'No. Amn't asked.' She looked over meaningly.

'We'll have to alter that. I often come. My sister and I are fond of the theatre.'

She couldn't allow this to pass without the conventional twitting.

'Your sister—?'

'Yes, really.'

He was surprisingly affected by her challenge. But, yes, of course, she had known that it was true. She had but meant the teasing to flatter and engage him. She smiled and echoed, 'Really!'

'Do you know, I haven't been out with girls much; usually I've gone places with Betty or my other sister,

Jane. I never seemed to get the chance to do anything else.'

'No west-end park for you, eh?'

'Well, I suppose I wanted to and thought myself a devil to try. But it always ended there.'

'Really?'

'Yes.'

The slightest twist to her lips brought a sudden and total change upon her face.

'What on earth are you thinking?' he asked quickly, almost in alarm.

But he knew what it was and he knew when she turned to answer that she was going to evade it. The lips were smooth again.

'When thieves turn honest,' she murmured.

'What then?'

'. . . they minimize their spoils.'

'Not very honest, then.'

'Are thieves ever?'

'In that case your thought's not just, for I am being honest.'

With a quick gesture she rejoined, 'There, I believe you.'

There was no attempt at girlish magnanimity in her expression, but he paid little thought to that. Aware, by a sudden divination she little suspected, of the actual process of her mind, he saw into the conclusion of her thought as though his eyes had been dazzling lights fixed upon hers. He knew she had meant him to see that sneer torturing her beautiful lips. She had meant it as an escape of contempt for this pompous discussion of his harmless babyish phil-andering of which she herself had tasted. She had meant it to establish a corner of uncertainty, of mystery, as alluring as the lips it had disfigured. Her covering up pretence of a belief that he had not noticed was expertly done.

'So,' his mind whispered into itself, 'thieves who turn

honest!' The words were like shadowing wings as he followed her along the ranks of knees to their seats again.

When he learned that she had no time for supper or for idling after the theatre he felt that Clifford had betrayed him. 'It's an awful bore, but I'm required at home,' she said; 'Mother's unwell and there's things to do.' They walked down to the railway bridge at Argyle Street, where they boarded a tram which took them to Peel Street, Partick, and Jessie's home in Black Street was only some five minutes' walk away. She lived with her father and mother in a tenement house in this district of lower-middle-class Glasgow whose jagged edges connect with Broomhill and Hyndland, select areas whose definitive name is the West End. Jessie, living in Partick, was well within her geographical rights when she said she lived 'out west'; but to withhold the name of Partick was to be purposefully misleading.

They parted almost immediately at the close mouth. He kissed her furtively several times and she pressed him to her then with quick embraces while making a little mystery of her desire to thank him for their lovely evening together. He whispered, 'Next week again?' and she answered joyously, 'Oh yes, do write, and tell me about it.' With that she left him. He heard her light steps patter up the stairs and then he drifted toward Dumbarton Road, whence they had come. Turning round between the luminous points of two lamp-posts he saw a window flash suddenly into existence upon the dark hulk of the tenement building, high up, a lonely peep of light below the chimneys in that gusty street. A sense of security quickened his thought and he stood looking about him. It was a dismal shallow place. It was not so much an assembly of homes as a huge dormitory in a wing of an immense factory. That window, illumined now by a greenish gasmantle, was of the apartment known as the parlour or the big room. It would be Jessie's room, where she would sleep in a concealed bed, a box cut into the wall like a press. During the daytime the door of the bed would be closed to keep the room tidy, and there the family would eat and sit about and smoke.

He kept his eye on the window until he was back at the close mouth. He wanted to examine the close so that he would be better able to imagine her comings and goings afterwards. No. 29. The number was printed on a blue tinplate on the stone outside and repeated on the painted panel within. The place was uncomfortably moist. A dark line of footmarks divided the whitewashed flags that led to the stairs. An unprotected electric globe, projected on ugly fittings, hung over the first steps and above the door in the close. It made an ineffectual glare in the surrounding gloom and had no impression whatever on a yawning gap, unutterably black, beneath the staircase on the left.

Nosing around, David could make no decision on the place until, when he stumbled upon the unseen steps at the entrance to that black space, he almost capsized and went staggering forward to clutch ultimately at a barred door. This treacherous recess, where he had stood with her on their first meeting, gave out to the common green and dustbins. He leaned against the wall and lighted a cigarette. He would have his spirit search the place. He was as alert as an animal whose sense of danger is aroused. Probably it was his imagination working some ill upon him in that dunny with its smell of middens, its moisture and utter dark; it might be quite different in the daytime. Just now it gave him intimations remote and unsettling. Her face was vivid to him and her lips had that cruel swift smile, like a little black sore. 'When thieves turn honest,' she had murmured. With no thought that he should remember it, she had included herself in its meaning, and now it seemed that this place was full of its echo.

She had been thinking of him flirting with her in his timid way, which he had thought so adventurous at the

time, and her sneer hinted at other experiences which
made his weak philandering a toying with precious time.
. . . This dunny!

Far above him in the hollow staircase there was the
sound of a door banging shut and a flurry of feet began
on the stairs. To be discovered loafing here was out of the
question; he had to clear away at once.

On tiptoe he found the three black steps and then hastened through the narrow passage to the street. Once there
and in comparative safety he wished to see who it was that
had disturbed him. So he stood on the roadway where the
close mouth narrowed his angle of vision to the stairway,
and waited. The steps quickened as they drew nearer, and
in a flash he saw a girl, wearing a blue print overall, slipping
round from the lighted stair into the dunny he had vacated.
She was carrying an ashpan heaped with refuse for the
midden. It was Jessie.

She had disappointed him in her eagerness to be gone,
especially when he had glimpsed that smile which seemed
to promise all that Clifford asserted was bound to be his.
Now, however, the evil impression of her smile was all
but obliterated by a second impression wholly good and
generous. Now he understood her haste to be gone. She was
anxious to get at the household work allotted to her, and
the sight of her skipping downstairs in that homely garment
linked her up with a domestic life he understood which was
outside the ambit of Clifford's thought.

These two conflicting impressions gave him a feeling of
having spent the night alone. He became detached from her
as he had been detached from the scene on the stage, and as
he wandered down Dumbarton Road and into Argyle Street
he remained aloof from his surroundings. Street lights were
glittering with but the tiniest halo of their own diffusion
encircling them, and all seemed to strike at the dark with
the sharpness of a note struck upon some instrument and

immediately muted. The pavements were uniformly grey
and dry save for spaces where shopkeepers had pitched the
water which had scoured their floors at closing-time. Trams
and 'buses went past with unirradiating rows of lights and
an inner sensation of moving passengers. But, though the
trams and 'buses were full, the crowds on the streets were
thinning down, and by the time he reached Jamaica Street
and turned south for Glasgow Bridge policemen on points-
duty were becoming prominent as rocks stand out when
the tide recedes. No aspect of the city's life was new to
David, but his impressions were profoundly affected by
his mood of complete detachment. He was tantalized by the
thought that there were unsuspected symbols in the orderly
processions of daily life. He had missed all these. The first
he had noticed was Jessie's smile. He imagined wide worlds
of feeling and adventure whose entrances were as secretive
as that quick cruel twist of her lips.

At Jamaica Street corner he boarded a tram. Immediately
in front of him a young fellow and a girl climbed the steps
to the upper deck, and the girl's silk stockings shone in the
glare of street and tram lights converging on the steps. There
was something in the confederate fashion of silk stockings
a man didn't fully realize. Something that drew him to the
verge of hidden pits of self. No one he had ever seen could
wear clothes better than Jessie: no one had such beautiful
limbs. Wasn't that sufficient for him? Let her smile mean
what it might; if it were good or if it were evil he would be
triumphant over it.

He soon found that he had been all wrong about the
smile. It came to her lips again and again during the
next few meetings, summoned by the most ordinary topics.
Clifford's name could bring it, just as Clifford's name
brought a slight superior sniff from Elizabeth; mention
of his office could bring it, or of his Uncle James, or
of his married sister's motor-car. None of these, though

uninspiring, could occasion ugly thoughts or wilful feelings. He came to the conclusion that her smile was a conscious attempt to express herself as superior to all these, and was ugly because it failed in this. It was not an important symbol of her character.

One day he said to her, 'I was busy last night helping the housekeeper. We cleaned out the sitting-room and my place. You should have seen the stuff I took out to the midden. I left a trail behind me on the garden path.'

'Getting ready for Christmas?' she smiled.

'No. I'm wanting the house to be nice for the time when I take you home for tea.'

She smiled at him then, her eyes lighting up with pleasure. The little hated smile would never malform her lips when he said so frank a thing as this. The expression of her mouth was simple and gracious. She had been waiting to see what he had meant, hoping perhaps that he loved her, but prepared in any event to be agreeable. Her smile might be more than a defensive sally against his possible philandering.

He had hoped this mention of cleaning rooms would start her off talking of her own home; but it did not. Her silence troubled him. He winced as he thought of her feelings had she discovered him watching her go down to the midden with the ashes. No one likes to be spied upon. Yet there it was: that secret sight of her changed everything. It gave him a strange power in his thoughts of her. Sometimes when she spoke grandly, with a touch of the salon gush of Bessie Fowlis, or when she waved her arms dramatically, making every movement an auxiliary emphasis of her words, he sat back in a secret content saying inwardly, 'It's all right, my lady; but tonight you'll be downstairs with ashes for the midden.' He smiled at the thought that her efforts to impress by gesticulating hand and eyebrow were made venial by his having spied behind their theatricality to the decent reality there. All of us, he thought, indulge the foibles of others on account of the better qualities behind.

And that she possessed those better qualities he was quickly finding out. Every day Clifford's influence exercised itself upon him so that at night he went seeking out Jessie only to have his ultimate aim gently frustrated or removed farther into the future. She was agreeable to him, quick with her kisses and as eager as he for the dark lanes behind Charing Cross, where they might stand unseen and undisturbed for hours. But there was a last defence which was unassailable, and in it she took responsibility for them both. Repeatedly when he was seeing her home or when they were parting, she would say, 'You've to thank me for keeping my head.' Which was not at all what Clifford prophesied. But then there might come that little wounding smile on her lips and he would go home unsure and unsettled.

It was impossible to tell Clifford all this. Clifford made him feel that no last line of defence would exist if he were there. It was a matter of aptitude. David became miserable upon the thought and looked at Clifford for the first time in a jealous hatred. But following this, when his behaviour with Jessie perhaps reflected it in an increased rashness and impetuosity, she triumphed anew. She responded in an equal impetuosity with an expression of faith in him, as though she were the custodian of a treasure belonging to both. It was as though she said, 'But it is ours; you can't steal it; you can only destroy it.' Nevertheless it was his if he must. And if he must, he would show that he thought it was his only and he would be betraying her. All the sacrifice would be with her.

With no words spoken she communicated this to him in his arms, and he realized her difference. He could not and he never would be able to overthrow such scruple. By a gesture the girl was safe again while unknown to her his mind had soared away. It had been lifted by a sudden rise of his mother's face upon his dawning love for this girl. His mother had come to countenance her upon this moment of her triumph over him. He recognized the vision as vividly as on former occasions, but it had no attendant fear. It was a smiling face. And that, after all, was the work of his own dexterous mind. He had to summon her face as his moral chart and give it light to countenance the girl who had survived his evil and brought him back, with a rush of tender feeling and admiration, to his normal self. That night on the way home he knew he would never escape his mother's face again. Now, indeed, because of Clifford and this girl, her province would be extended so that she would dispense judgment not only on those domestic matters she had once known, but on the entire scheme and substance of his life.

Soon he was meeting Jessie at some hour each day, contriving, if they were not to be together in the evening, to see her for a brief space before tea-time or at lunch. After these daytime glimpses of her, when she was restless to be gone or had a preoccupied air, he feared that her feelings had not been deeply stirred for him. He would leave her then in a growing despondency which became obvious as the afternoon wore on, and at coffee-time Clifford might twit him. Was he not making progress with Jessie? He might admit it. Or had he got himself involved? At that he could shake his head. The thing was so different from what Clifford had in mind.

She would probably be a most efficient worker in the shop, he mused. The shop was a reality to her: it was inescapable and afforded no scope for little affectations and deceits. While she was working, and during her lunch-hour, she was in commission, and social frills were suspended like an evening gown laid away.

'You are so different at night, Jessie.' he said to her once when they had met to spend the long evening together. She was freshened from the work of the shop by all the aids of modern toilet and deeply enwrapped by a heavy tweed coat which softened into lines of fur at pockets and cuffs and skirt.

'Different?' She loved to hear herself discussed.

'During the daytime you're like a captive out on leave. But at night you look as though you owned the world.'

'A captive? Well, you must liberate me!'

'I wish I could!' he whispered.

They were in a café attached to a picture house in town. A jazz band played noisily while a young attendant, dressed like a miniature waiter, went slowly round the room bearing the number of the item on a large placard. Patrons had but to look at the programme on the table to be made musically up to date. People all round hummed and ate chocolate biscuits.

She leaned forward, and the brim of her hat touched his forehead. Quickly he drew back and then carefully judged the infinity that separated them over a patch of table. But she did not seem to notice the risk she had taken of attracting unpleasant attention. A quiet had come upon her, her eyes were mild and shadowy.

It was the moment he would have to use, but it came so suddenly, its excitement created by a twist in their ordinary talk, that he was taken aback. He smiled in an attempt at ease and took up the music programme.

'Number ten,' he murmured.

The place was unbearably bright and rowdy. Her eyes, shaded by the big brim of her hat, were pools of quiet. As he hesitated, memory, like a separate chamber from all this, seemed to throw open its doors and all the phrases he had thought over came in on him, jumbled and confused. This was no place to marshal them. This was no place to tell her that she did not really belong to gay and frivolous places, to tearooms and the garish street.

He wanted to tell her that he did not care for her little tricks of manner, her hints of worldly wisdom. It seemed good news he had to tell, as though on his admission that he loved her hidden self she would be able to tear away a mask that irked her. But it now became the most difficult thing in the world to say.

The music programme had a blank page at the end with the title 'Extra' at the top. He folded it at this page and with his pen he wrote her name. Their heads were close now, but it didn't matter.

'Well?' she murmured when this was done.

With all those thoughts tumbling uselessly in his mind, he wrote down, slowly and deliberately, 'I love you.'

She made no sign, sitting still and looking at those three words as though they were a picture of infinite detail. Then, without looking up, her hand took his pen and she added his name and below it his words.

Both of them gazed intently on this enlargement. The slanting loops of her letters gave the page the appearance of a wind having blown across it.

Once more he took the pen, and scoring out the word 'Extra' with the utmost precision he substituted 'Our Covenant', and then, below her blown words he wrote: 'And for ever'. The pen came slowly towards her fingers. It was great fun! Very firmly and boldly she wrote: 'For ever and evermore.'

PART THREE

Jessie

When Jessie was no more than eighteen she was known to every waitress in Sauchiehall Street's succession of tearooms. It was in one of these she met David, and they had thrown up her previous friends, some fleeting and some difficult to shake off. Jessie, however, had known the difference immediately with David. He was not like the others. He could not be impressed as the others were, and yet one could do pretty much what one liked with him. Jessie had been an amateur actress for several years now and had appeared in all the recent shows of the Ringside Players. In this environment she conceived it necessary to gesticulate with hand and eyebrow and develop as an essential part of her much that at the beginning had been mere affectation. David seemed able to penetrate this, which she was pleased to call 'veneer', and that was why she was not quite sure of herself in the daytime. At night, in the bright light of tearooms or in the darkened lanes, it was different. There she could arrange for her little wordy explosions—'Gracious, darling, how could you!' or 'Aw, I say, how perfectly marvellous!'—and control her voice in its downward swoop into a veritable flood of words. There she had the aid of colours and shadows and the dark.

There was no doubt that she was pretty and attractive. She was almost as tall as David, with delicately shaped shoulders that her dress served to emphasize. Her face looked out on the world, as it looked into her mirror, under the arch of a hat shaped Quakerwise, with ribbons running round it and fluttering to an end over the traces of bobbed hair at the back. It was a pleasing face with a childlike simplicity which, for all her histrionics, prevailed on those she met to treat her amiably.

For the past five years she had never been without the prospect of marriage. She could divide her memories into sections such as 'It was Bobby Rutherford then' or 'It was Francis then' or 'That was Jacky Millar or Tom Muir'. Something had happened in each case, however, and these young fellows had gone on their several ways. For the first year or two her confidence had been untroubled, but ultimately she watched them depart with an almost fatalistic solemnity. They were amiable to the last, and even after it was all over some of them remained chummy. She met them in tearooms occasionally or at parties or rehearsals, where they were extremely polite, conscious of the gratuitous experience their affairs with her had been. But they went no more home with her and took no part in her life at all.

David had come in on her out of the dark. He was unknown to any of her friends except Bessie Fowlis and uninterested in any of her amusements. Her affair with Tom Muir was just over—she had ben speaking of it to Bessie when David and Clifford had approached their table on that memorable night—and inwardly she had been tearful and unsettled. Then, suddenly, everything was changed. He had asked her to the theatre; he listened to her talk with a diffidence she had never before met with; he told her of his own life at home with his sister; of his married sister, Jane, and her two children; of Archie Duke, her husband, who had the posh shop in Sauchiehall Street; of his Uncle James and his stocks and shares; all this in a manner which presumed that she had the counterparts of these people in her own family. It was a strain to begin with, for she was never sure of saying the right thing. When he asked her questions about her home it did not occur to her to tell the truth. Her difficulty lay in creating an impression as favourable. She could not explain how dissatisfied she had been when his appearance lit up the prospect ahead and made all that had

gone before illusory. Yet she wanted to tell him that falling
in love with him had been like going away from everything
she had hitherto known. It had meant renunciation of those
things she said and did every day, renunciation too of
memories which, being unsuspected by him, seemed now
illegally in her possession. It was no excuse that they meant
nothing to her; their very meaninglessness was an affront.
But these things she did and said every day persisted: they
were renounced only in the mind. She continued in the
scenes and amid the people of her earlier loves and failures.
The black background of her home remained unchanged,
and she feared that when he came to see it he would be
repelled as Bobby Rutherford had been repelled when he
visited her unexpectedly one day. Bobby, of course, would
never have admitted this, but she knew it in her heart and
she didn't blame him.

Her job was to keep David away from the house, and
this she contrived to do very successfully. But one night
they went bang into her father and the whole situation was
charged with danger.

He was waiting for her outside the rehearsal rooms
where the committee were casting a new play. It was
raining heavily when she emerged, and David, seizing her
umbrella, opened it and swept her underneath. She hugged
his arm excitedly.

'I've got a glorious part!' she cried. 'I'm to play lead
opposite Jimmy Crane. Isn't it great!'

'Marvellous! I see you living in Hollywood some day if
the film folk hear of it.'

'And it's going on in six weeks, too,' she continued. 'I'll
have so much to do.'

Suddenly her tone changed, and as though to meet his
disappointment she assumed a bland unconcern.

'I must go straight home tonight.'

'Oh, but you can't!' he complained.

'I'm afraid I've no choice. Heavens! what a night.'

The rain was running from the umbrella in streams. The backs of her silk stockings were drenched.

'What a hopeless rig-out for a night like this,' he observed as he glanced at her unprotected costume and slim shoes.

'I know. I wasn't home for tea, and at lunch-time the weather was fine.'

'Perhaps, then, it's just as wise for you to go straight home.'

He said this slyly, for he remembered that when she was mysterious as now, and threatening his happiness, she invariably had some pleasant scheme in mind.

'Only,' he added, 'you'd better have a cup of tea first.'

'No,' she replied firmly, 'you'll have to take me home now.'

The way she said this set him thinking. Perhaps she was inviting him to supper. She would have it all arranged: her mother expecting them at a certain hour and everything ready. It was a nice idea which he pretended not to have anticipated.

'It must be fun to act in a play,' he said admiringly; 'I simply haven't got it in me.'

'Oh, we're only amateurs, you know; but it is nice.'

'There's so many of you nowadays, though. The time's coming when there won't be any audiences at all: nothing but players!'

'It's terrible,' she said feelingly, 'you should see some of the folk who apply for membership. They can't speak properly.'

'It makes you wonder, doesn't it?'

'Oh, awfully.'

By this time they were approaching Wellington Street tram stop, and lowering the umbrella they made for the shelter of La Scala doorstep. David gazed into the brightly lit and comfortable tearoom beyond the vestibule. 'What about it?' he asked, nodding appreciatively inwards and shivering. Then he caught sight of an odd look in her eyes.

'Is there anything wrong?' he queried. She shook her head quickly and looked past him into the tearoom.

He felt a curious sensation of having been cut off. He stood beside her and was abandoned by her. 'Jessie,' he whispered, 'what has happened?'

She turned slowly. 'All right,' her voice was no more than a murmur, 'let us have some tea.'

But on the instant of this being said David discovered its reason. His eyes had shot round him and were confronted by the gaze of a man standing at the extreme edge of the doorway. He was a burly man, late in middle life, and of an appearance of vagrancy refuted only by the look in his eyes. Hardly conscious of how he came about it, David knew the man to be Jessie's father.

'Won't you come?' There was a slight hardness in her voice now.

He avoided her eyes.

'Why, no Jessie; perhaps we shouldn't. You're drenched and better get home.' He saw the man, who had a full view of the street, turn up his collar and step down to the pavement. A yellow tramcar swung along. 'Anyway, here's the car.'

He was certain now. Giving her no chance to remonstrate, he pushed open the umbrella and they made a dive for the tram.

The burly fellow was the only other passenger getting on, and as he stopped on the platform to give the conductor his fare his back was to the youngsters, who climbed quickly on top. Perhaps, David thought, he will stay inside. But Jessie knew he would not. Her sparkle was extinguished, leaving the dullness of timidity on her spirit. She was as forlorn as a child discovered at a forbidden game.

As luck would have it, there was no other person on the upper deck. It was the quiet hour before the theatres and cinemas skailed. They settled themselves on a seat midway and waited, he in a growing expectancy and she in a sickness of dread. Then came the inevitable encounter when the glass door was slung open and shut (to be opened almost immediately by the conductor, who came for David's pennies). Jessie's nerve failed her and she whispered, 'Just take penny ones.' Her father was lurching past them, turning round slowly and going through the pantomime of discovering his daughter on the same tram. He threw over the back of the next seat and sat down opposite them.

Immediately he looked as though he had been pitched there by a violent jolt of the vehicle and must stick until he rotted. One of his thighs trespassed the girl's slim knee and the other squeezed against David's, with a foot protruding rigidly into the passage. His eyes, small and dark, surveyed his daughter listlessly, while a dampness at one corner of his mouth was poked at ineffectually by an unhealthy tongue. Anything less like the father of a society amateur actress could hardly be imagined.

David's first effort, in a flush of magnanimity, was to stir up recollections of characters whose ungainly exterior hid a life of benevolence and good offices, and acting upon the conviction that this man must belong to such an order he became valiantly affable.

But long years of concentration in business had caused Mr Adair to neglect his social qualities as well as his person. Or was it that, having few occasions in which to appear agreeable, he had lost the faculty, and, having grown stout, had come to think his carriage not worth troubling about? His clothes were shapeless and creased, his face pale and blemished, his voice a mere thread.

'Your mother's worried about your clothes.' He spun this out slowly and with every appearance of asthmatic difficulty.

'I'm all right,' Jessie said. She turned hesitantly to David, a flush on her cheeks. 'This is my father,' she murmured.

'One couldn't tell it was going to be such a dreadful night,' David said almost too brightly. 'It was quite pleasant early on.'

The man did not look at him.

'These shoes are lettin' in, she says.'

'No, they're not!'

The irritation of this was torturous. Jessie dreaded the outcome of it all. When the car swung round Charing Cross she began nudging David's elbow with dots and dashes he could make nothing of. He knew she was on tenterhooks and felt sorry for her, and once he turned with a smile of assurance and a wink. But the excitement of the meeting had estranged her, and her glance was as cold on him as on her father. When the car reached the Art Galleries she made a definite movement to rise and David got quickly to his feet.

Lifting his hat to the old fellow, he waited till Jessie, who left without a word, had sidled past into the passage, and then courteously took his leave. After all, this was his future father-in-law. But no such yielding thoughts were in the other's head. When Jessie scrambled out of the seat, made hazardous by her father's thighs, perhaps her own were momentarily unveiled, or her dress in some way disturbed. David could not tell. Whatever had happened, the man had eyes only for her legs as he hunched himself up in the seat to look after her.

'Oh, David!' There was something fugitive in the involuntary exclamation: it was the very shivering of the soul.

David took her arm swiftly and pressed it.

'What's up?'

He knew that from her heart she was grateful for this. A wave of warmth from her swept over him as her fingers dug feverishly into his sleeve. It was with difficulty he swung open the umbrella to protect her shoulders from the driving rain.

'I thought you might not have liked my father,' she murmured.

Liked? It hadn't occurred to him. 'Why shouldn't I?'

'I dunno,' she sighed, and shook her head sadly.

'I'm afraid he'll think it queer of us getting off the car here.'

'Let him. I don't care what he thinks.'

'He seems a harmless soul, Jessie. I thought you were rather hard on him.'

'Have to be. Got to watch him.'

'What does he do? You've never told me.'

'He's an agent.'

'Furs, or something like that?'

She nodded.

'Does he take much interest in your friends?'

'Father? None. He's got no social sense.' Then, on a sudden resolve to be dramatic: 'Dear knows what he's got. I'm tired to death of him.'

'I say, Jessie!'

'Yes, I know all you can tell me, darling; duty and the rest of it.' Here she released his arm to get the full use of expressive hands. 'But it's no use. He's the damnedest wretch.'

'But, Jessie dear, this is terrible.'

'Isn't it just!'

They walked on, overcome by the immensity of her admission. He thought of Elizabeth. She would be at Isa Cummings' tonight. A number of Isa's friends met once a week to take lessons in sewing. Some of them were teachers who had already had classes in sewing. But when they saw Elizabeth's work they wanted more. He thought of Jane in that trim villa at Prestwick, sitting reading at the fireside now that the children were safely tucked under the blankets. There was something lovely in the idea of a mother sitting at the fire in a cosy room when the children were asleep upstairs.

'Surely he doesn't ill-use you, darling?' His tone was incredulous and tender.

Jessie sighed in pity for herself at this too sudden complication of her affairs. She didn't want this. It was precipitating things beyond, far beyond the present scheme.

'That's why it's so desperately hard to leave you at night, David,' she murmured. 'It wasn't so bad before, somehow. But now I can scarcely stand it.'

'I never dreamt—'

'No.' She sighed again and he was afraid to say more.

They made straight for Black Street, and reached No. 29 shortly before ten o'clock. He expected her to leave immediately; but she was still aglow with the warmth he had felt when they left the tramcar, and she made no sign of parting. They stood irresolutely for a moment and then her hand clasped his. 'Come in,' she whispered, and she led him on tiptoe through the close to the black space under the stairs.

Entirely safe, she reminded him; no one ever passed through to the back green at night. Would he stand with his back to the wall, that way; and would he hold her, like this, and kiss her? Her movements were light and stealthy, her voice but a breath on his cheek.

'Did you think I really wanted to be home early, dear?' she whispered.

'I wondered,' he replied softly.

'You dear. I wanted to bring you here, out of the rain.' She seemed to melt into his arms. 'I'm so weary, David.'

It was eleven o'clock when he let her go. He stood at the close mouth while she slowly climbed the stairs backwards, holding to the banister with one hand and throwing kisses with the other. Once he took a run and leaped up the steps and they kissed again, and again the slow process of widening the distance between them began, this time by his retreating out of the close. It was hard to let her go. It was desperately hard when you didn't know the kind of house she was going to. It was unspeakably hard when you yourself were going back to a house that was safe and warm and beautiful.

The rain had stopped, but there were no stars, and a piercing wind blew along that shabby street. He buttoned up his coat and made for Dumbarton Road, where he boarded a red tram.

His mind fed upon the substance of its excitement all the way into town. It seemed incredible that this elation would ever pass away. He felt that if he looked down on normal life now he would be sick as though suspended over a precipice. He was a lover and a liberator. A lover on whose path moral obstacles had suddenly sprung up, alluring him to a test of strength. These obstacles were the very need of his love, and a tenderness for Jessie vindicated the pleasurable vanity in his strength. His mind was imparadised in the thought that he could take her away and make her happy. She was so obviously fitted to be happy. An eagerness of spirit flowed over her, revealing rather than hiding her essential shyness. It was like the water of a shallow stream, pleasantly sunlit. Everything was plain and obvious to him now.

Nevertheless, when his excitement died down it was upon a strangely apprehensive mind. He got home thoroughly soaked, took off his shoes and lay back in a chair at the fire. Elizabeth was sewing at the other side. He looked at her wonderingly for a time.

'I say, Betty, would you mind if I brought someone here for tea soon?'

'Someone? I'd like that very much.'

'She's sort of unhappy as far as I can see. It's all come out rather suddenly. She's really a sweet girl but her folk seem strange. I met her old man tonight. He doesn't look up to much. Yet she talks of them quite decently. It's tough luck.'

Elizabeth had put her sewing to one side and was now gazing into the fire, her fingers whirling a thimble.

'What's her name?'

'Jessie Adair.'

'Nice name.'

It was difficult for Elizabeth. He talked as though the thing were well advanced, yet this was the first she had heard of it. And he was not in a mood to be chaffed.

'I'll have everything beautiful for her,' she said, 'as soon as you like.'

For Jessie the prospect of visiting Cornfoot Avenue was almost as unpleasant as the memory of David's meeting with her father. In the one case she was disturbed by jealous fears and in the other by shame. David made much ado about the visit. It was an event to quicken their love-making, and there was the suggestion in it of a new shelter should she become too vexed by her father. To be sure, David did not speak slightingly of her parent, and she had resumed her manner of loyal silence or presumption of equality; but there was a note of confidence, a promise of warmth and comfort in all David said of his own home. Everyone, he told her, was pleasantly expectant: Elizabeth was busying herself getting the house in order; Jane had written saying she was also coming for tea, and Uncle James, who had heard about it, was coming along if he were free of business engagements. Archie Duke had phoned congratulating him and inviting them both down to Prestwick. They all believed Jessie would be characteristic of him. 'I expect she's awfully Davish,' Elizabeth had laughed.

Jessie listened to all this with little joy. But there was just the hope that she would be able to fit into the illusion of her that his talk and reputation had created. She might, indeed, ultimately learn to act the 'Davish' business they expected of her. That would take time, however, and be dependent upon her successful behaviour meantime.

He met her in town when the night came and took her to the house. All the way on the tram and while walking up Cornfoot Avenue she was seeking confidence from him and working intuitively on his replies to her whispered fears. 'I'm so afraid they won't like me,' 'I'm timid of meeting people, really,' 'What like is Uncle James to strangers?'

'This is silly of you,' he exclaimed at last. 'Why, they'll all love you. Elizabeth especially is terribly excited. They'll be as nervous as you, I expect.'

But he was exaggerating. Jessie had affected him by her uneasiness, and now that the meeting was imminent he was discovering secret fears of his own. He remembered the night he had come home from the first encounter, soiled by a taste of lip-salve and ginger ale and with the smell of cheap scent in his nostrils. His bedroom had been cool and clean. The house had been wrapped in silence with Elizabeth at its core, and he had felt himself an intruder bringing unwholesome airs about him. That was his first impression. Would the first impression now about to be made on others be vastly different? As he answered her fears with bright assurances he was consoling himself with the thought that Jessie was keyed up to the event and displaying none of her tearoom gush.

Long afterwards he was convinced that the apprehension they both shared on that night had been a poison which communicated itself to the others. In the last analysis, the failure of the meeting lay with Jessie; but how much of her unsympathetic responses, her hardness, due to fright, her subtle underrating of the social sense of her neighbours, might not have been missed had they both been buoyant in confidence? First, for Jessie, it was the lighted hall, Maisie's murmur and guidance to the wide heavily carpeted stairs, and then the broad landing on which a door opened, throwing a flood of light about her. Then a clear voice greeted her and in it the dissolution of all she had expected was complete. She walked into the lighted room as though it were a stage on which she had to play an unrehearsed part.

Her first effort to gain some kind of control of herself was a searching for that excitement which Elizabeth was said to have shown. When she could not find any trace of it her agitation increased. Elizabeth was viewing her with no preconceived admiration she was reluctant to dismiss. She stood at the fireplace, her feet embedded in the wool of a white hearthrug, her auburn head bright against a wall of palest cream, quiet and perfectly at ease. She was so used to encountering all kinds of people. Jessie met her eye in the mirror as she arranged her hair and powdered her nose. They smiled. Jessie's impulse then was to turn suddenly and break up her excitement in a wordy noise, but she restrained herself and waited on the other to move. There was a pause. 'Ready?' she was asked. It seemed that she had been taking ages before that mirror.

Immediately they were all together in the big room a triangle was formed which was to endure for many a day. All knew as time went on that the latent gladness of the night would never flower. Uncle James, beginning in a hearty welcome and with a genuine interest which occasioned his taking Jessie's hand in both of his and beaming upon her, settled into a bland mood against which David strove in vain. His sisters' blandness was not so cruel, for it was to some extent assumed. But Uncle James was disappointed, and, thinking that his falling-away in interest would not be noticed, he became dutifully polite and suave, inwardly acknowledging that it didn't matter to him. His nephew was just an ordinary boy with ordinary tastes.

Elizabeth and Jane were less cruel because they were more concerned. Yet when David's secret wrath was spent on his uncle it mounted higher than ever against them. Less cruel to their brother they were, but what shred of humanity had they for this girl whose heart was being bruised by their manner? It was ruthless snobbery. It was the snobbery of Clifford intensified a hundred times. They were as certain of Jessie's inaptitude as Clifford had been of her virtue. They did not see her as he did, a little thing of fear, sensitive to hurt, excited like a squirrel in a light. They were coldly, calmly intent upon the performance of a social duty and yielded nothing to the need of their inexperienced guest.

Ultimately Jessie, rising from her chair, broke into a pause that had come in the conversation and been allowed to expand unbearably. She would have to go, she said; she was expected home early as her mother was ill. For the few minutes which followed before they went upstairs to the bedroom, there was a hint of warmth in Elizabeth's manner. Jessie got a glimpse then, as though looking down an opened corridor, of reaches she would never be allowed. Her hat and coat were swiftly donned and she was back at David's side.

Going down Cornfoot Avenue, the atmosphere of the room lingered upon them. Touched by Elizabeth's momentary kindliness, which had been but an expression of relief at her going, Jessie said humbly, 'Elizabeth's lovely. She must be great when you get to know her.'

It was the feeling she had of looking down a vista unexplored.

'Yes,' he answered, 'I suppose she's nice enough. But she's got very little feeling, really.'

'Oh, no,' Jessie protested, 'I'm sure she's terribly kind. But—but I couldn't just be at ease, somehow.—They're awfully nice.'

'You were wonderful,' he said simply, knowing she wanted this assurance. And all the way over to Partickhill he was called on to say it again and again.

When he returned home he found his sister at the fire alone. She was sewing, and did no more than look up when he entered. He had known she would make no sign. She would not translate her disappointment into anything challengeable. It was betrayed only by the absence of an expectant glow. So well he knew her, he was bored by her calm.

'It's almost midnight,' she said, 'but this has to be finished for the morning.'

'Sorry if you've been kept back,' he said bitterly, watching her fingers.

She made no rejoinder to this, but passed on blithely enough to what was perhaps evoked by it. 'I'll have to get busy on the family poem soon, eh? I must ask Jessie if it's a teacloth she wants, like Jane's.'

'Huh!' Weariedly he turned aside. Like Jane's! How all unconsciously her voice had honeyed at that name. Jane and she had sat here talking after Uncle James had gone; they had talked while Elizabeth had stitched until their subject was dropped, as Elizabeth's sewing was dropped, on Jane's sudden exclamation, 'I must fly for my train!' David felt their talk in the air and could have pulled out the phrase 'He's a silly ass' from the atmosphere as easily as he could have lifted a cushion from a chair.

He left her at her work, but it was a long time before he slept. She was downstairs working with nimble fingers on dazzling linen, but soon she too would go to bed. Until she did the house would remain tense. He waited, and at long last he heard her door shut quietly, and it seemed that immediately the tension relaxed and the ease of sleep descended on the house. He knew well enough she was right. All that she inevitably said to Jane had been right. Jessie had not impressed, though she had not betrayed him. She had not betrayed him, for instance, by that torturous smile. He knew of that smile and Elizabeth didn't. He had seen her father and heard him talk and Elizabeth hadn't. There were indeed reasons for—yes, for disliking her, but neither Elizabeth nor Jane nor Uncle James knew aught of them. Were they fair to her, then? How dare they be so cruel to a little creature because she gave them an obvious measure of their own superiority?

His thoughts turned guiltily to his own first intentions with Jessie. She was to have been his experiment with what Clifford called 'life'.

He had planned, with no thoughts of her feelings, to use her as cruelly, if in a different and more popular way. He had been no better than they were now. Only this, she had prevailed upon him. His decency had been more vulnerable than her virtue. And when he had seen her with the ashpan, hurrying somewhat furtively to the midden, he had perceived her life to be as authentic as his own. He pictured the close in Black Street, suggesting as it did, with its dark stairs and faint repugnant smell, the bleakness of her daily routine. She took him to her in the darkness of that close, giving him her happy kisses and warm embraces with no thought other than of the delight she was bringing him. She was proud in her kisses as she never was in her dresses and station. Proud little creature who knew so well the pleasure she could give him and the pleasure she could promise that was greater still. Was she not right in her pride, was she not vindicated, as he was, in going on, by the unspeakable sweetness of her kisses, of her womanhood, revealed to him alone? What did anything else matter beside that?

At the breakfast table he looked like a child from whose hands Elizabeth had removed a toy. There came a vivid onrush of childish petulance, with a loosening of tears at the throat. Between them then there sprang up an old forgotten antagonism which had once existed over the barest of material things. Now, after many years, he was the younger brother recalcitrant again and with daggers in his eyes.

And she, normally composed and tranquil, revealed once only her awareness of his inward agitation, once when, with a peculiar movement of her head, she glanced at the door connecting the dining-room with the study. There was a look in her eyes then that had been of terrible meaning to him long ago, when after some raid or row they were shepherded at table awaiting their father, she to see her rights established, he to be chided or dispossessed. In those far-off days her look had been sad and almost maternal in its softness, yet her intent had been ruthlessly cruel.

That look was in her eyes again. It was a temporary fluttering of the spirit seeking aid from a familiar quarter on a renewal of old familiar conflict.

But no father came to rebuke the boy, though for an immeasurable moment his senses were suspended awaiting the closed door's opening. Then a drift of tears went over his mind and a nostalgic sickness followed.

He made no attempt to 'vindicate' Jessie to Elizabeth or to have her vindicate herself. He accepted her and purposefully narrowed his vision until she and her concerns occupied him wholly. Elizabeth's talk on domestic affairs became stale, like echoes from the past, and in a short time even Clifford ceased to trouble him. One afternoon he told Clifford that he and Jessie were 'different', and the intimation was so definite that Clifford, with a social sense as correct as Elizabeth's, dropped Jessie's name entirely from his casual talk. Jessie became more and more capable of a self-abandonment which elevated him to a permanent excitement in his physical being. But one day she revealed a hitherto hidden ambition, when in the humility of her attitude towards Elizabeth she told him she had made a new hat for herself. Later, when this was being worn and admired and nicknamed 'the silver crest', she stitched a camisole which she carried in her bag together with bobbins and needle. A cold snap came and she hurriedly knitted him a scarf in brown and golden wool. Then one evening, when he had been praising this, she asked, her voice quivering slightly, 'Does Elizabeth ever make things for you?' and he felt a pulling here that made all her attempts at millinery and embroidery plain. 'No,' he said, letting a little harshness enter his voice as hostility toward Elizabeth, 'she doesn't even think of such a thing.'

PART FOUR

Black Street

I

Until the spring came, all their time together was spent in the city, its restaurants and tearooms and cinemas, its quiet streets and shadowy lanes and open places. Jessie returned but once to Cornfoot Avenue and on that occasion stayed only a few minutes. The city and approachable suburbs satisfied them, and thoughts of home and the relevance of each other to home affairs dwindled away in the habits of city life.

When the weather advanced with the spring they took trips to the Eaglesham moors and to the meadowlands that lie between Busby and Carmunnock. On Saturday afternoons and on Sundays they went farther afield, adventuring, as it felt to them, on the shores of Loch Lomond or Loch Long, where they explored the steep woods above the railway line or sailed on the waters.

From every excursion of this kind they returned full of additional secrets of their love-making. The islets on Loch Lomond fascinated them, and although aware of the romantic names given them in the district they christened them with names of their own. The small woods and byways on the south side of Glasgow were similarly treated; a road stretching from Waterfoot to Thorntonhall they called 'Hedges', and a road half a mile removed from this, 'Rainy Road'; a tearoom in Eaglesham became 'Assisi Pancakes', for there they had seen a man eating pancakes and reading Mr Chesterton's book on St Francis. The zone of their loving became etched upon the map by a secret list of fanciful names.

But daily drudgery such as she had known before she met David persisted for Jessie. All this happiness was separate from her permanent self, which continued in places he knew nothing about. Her happiness could not penetrate the mind and steep it in a glow of tolerance and sweetness, lighting up everywhere she went; rather was it an extrinsic influence directing her to rebellious thoughts and resolutions of escape. In the mornings, in her concealed bed in the parlour—it was a small room and the door of the bed, thrown open, almost touched the table at the centre of the floor—she lingered, unrefreshed by sleep which had been but an interruption of her hold on life. She would lie on until the gleam of her next meeting with David brightened up her prospect sufficiently to rouse her. Then she would get up, dress and go out to her work. This business of rising and dressing and going out to her work and of standing behind a counter all day was like a long road she had to travel if she were to get to him. Walking up Buchanan Street she would see the morning skies reflected on high windows and look yearningly at some cloud pink-flushed and billowy far above her. The air was sweet even in Buchanan Street at that early hour, and as the spring wore on it seemed that the air was scented as though fields and gardens were but round the corner. The natural reaction of her young body to these mornings, the exhilaration in her blood, perplexed her. Turning into her shop, she would give the whole mystery of her feelings to her desire for David.

Morning after morning she thought of David leaving Cornfoot Avenue, a full hour after she had started work. There were trees in his avenue, and to have trees growing outside your windows was an extravagance of riches. She had often asked David if he noticed the opening buds on the branches, and his answers made up a picture of him walking down the avenue and glancing into the gardens and thinking of her. Servants were about the doors at that time, sweeping the steps and polishing the brasses, and milk-boys were returning to the dairies with jangle of empty cans.

He noticed these things, he said, because he was in love. And then he smiled sheepishly, for he couldn't explain why he should not have noticed them before. Once he said—it was in early March and the days were but dawning when he went into town—that he could not remember having seen dawn over Glasgow before. Of course he must have, many times. But everything was memorable now, now that he was in love. Had he been asked to speculate he'd have said that dawn over Glasgow was like an ungainly fellow clambering out of bed, whereas it was exquisitely delicate and gentle. He liked the prospect from Glasgow Bridge best of all; slate grey with a greyish mauve sky, iron bridges etched darkly upon a background of factories, and the river below unexpectedly light. The dawn like a quiet air seemed to creep along the surface of things, streets and river, and slowly rise to envelop the buildings and wharfs, cranes and bridges, until it lit up the sky.

He found everything memorable now, he said, and she sighed at the thought. Certainly the dawn, with the houses and bridges and wharfs reappearing in familiar shapes out of a grey mistiness, was a memorable sight, and certainly pink-flushed windows over the city buildings and fresh morning airs blowing down the streets were lovely experiences; but they were momentary, perishable and never twice alike. So much else of life, the routine customs of every day, exacting and tyrannical, was memorable by its deadly persistence.

These customs never varied: they were the permanent influence of which she was afraid. They were a continual menace to her love and therefore to her acceptance of pink windows and buds on suburban trees and fresh morning airs as well. Their force was sufficient to dispel all beauty from her mind so that they occupied it wholly. There was her father with his nagging and his unsociable manners; there was the deadening home atmosphere in which she existed, listlessly awaiting the hours that would summon her away;

there was the cruel impersonal supervision in the shop; and there were memories of other love affairs in which she had for various reasons failed to hit it off. The memories were perhaps the most forceful and crippling of all. They intruded upon the pleasant events with David so that in his voice she heard echoes and in his look she saw shadows from her unsuccessful past. At such moments she thought that all men were alike, and only with the corner of her eye, as it were, did she catch at something comical in her attitude of thus blaming the man. Assuredly they were not all alike. It was her capacity to make David react as other boys had reacted that brought about a surface likeness: that was all.

And it tortured her mind to think that this was so. No amount of sewing, of making new hats, of knitting or of reading books could cover the flaw in her which everyone sooner or later seemed to discover. Why was it, too, that although needlework was not the prerogative of Elizabeth, David should seem to think she was but studiously copying his sister and act tenderly towards her as towards a child? It was all an effort to hide rather than to change one's real self. But though she recognized this and feared it she did not understand why it should be so. She felt no evil towards anyone and had no malicious intent to deceive.

To be given a chance, that was what she wanted. And David was so negotiable that if they were left alone she was certain she would succeed. Yes, in spite of those shadows from the past upon him, she was certain. But they would never be left alone. All the influences she dreaded were directed by other people. People on his side and on hers. David and she might alter so that they required solitude; these people wouldn't see that, and would continue to exercise their selfishness upon them. He often asked her about her home, feeling that she was unhappy. He wanted to know so that he might sympathize. But that was not safe. A boy tires of being sympathetic. He wants companionship on an equal footing. He also wants the basis of that companionship to be nice. If David pried deep enough into her home affairs his sympathy might be overtaxed. He might feel himself implicated or threatened in something so nasty that he would back out altogether. So she put him off when he inquired and with wistful smiles murmured something like 'Don't let us be miserable: let's talk about ourselves,' in which he saw that she was afraid to speak and that she was worried.

'You know, darling,' she said once, 'being in love with you is like going away on holiday—away from everything. And as it's to last for ever, we should be going away for ever, to some new place. To a quiet place, with trees and sunshine. Can you understand?'

'I feel the same, dearest,' he whispered back. How wonderful of her to talk so, he thought. It was more beautiful than he could have imagined. All his life he had been led to expect that girls had reserves which were a mystery and a torment. But there was nothing of mystery remaining in Jessie. She was self-revealed and frank as the day. She spoke with no reserve of sex, while her sense of difference brought her closer to him than anyone had ever been.

She told him nothing of her home life, yet when something happened to her there, what could be more frank than her silent faith that he would comfort her? She was unhappy and ashamed. He saw that she was ashamed of being unhappy. And that was why she would not tell him. But one night when she came to him, dark-eyed and tearful, he knew she was agitated too deeply for his presence to soothe her, and in the end his questioning, a ritual with him, to which he expected evasive replies, broke down her barriers and she explained.

She had gone home that evening and asked her parents if she might get a new overcoat, a spring coat. She wanted it for the holiday, to wear when she was with David, she had said. 'Father growled at me. They are rather poor, you know. But I haven't had a coat for ages. Anyway, there was a flare-up.

Mother is in bed. She's still ill. And of course she got excited and blamed me. Then father blamed me for exciting her and making her worse. And so I won't get a coat, but I've a terrible atmosphere to endure.'

It was all outside the range of his experience, and yet how well he understood! There was nothing to do but envelop her more closely in his tender regard. A spring coat! Well, he couldn't give her that without them asking questions. But there might be other things he could do. Until she had spoken he had not noticed she needed a new coat. Once he had thought her dress expensive. But now as he shyly surveyed her he realized that he had known this long while of her need of things and had noted almost subconsciously the little deft adjustments by which she contrived a look of goodness to material worn bare or intrinsically poor. So one night when Elizabeth was out he went into her wardrobe and inspected her intimate laces and linen, and of them all, including silk stockings, he made a selection which he folded in a paper parcel and took to Jessie. Elizabeth's tolerance of her own carelessness was a certain shield.

'Here are some traveller's samples you might like,' he said to her. 'A man in the office was selling them today. I bought them for—my sister!'

They laughed shyly. They were sitting at the edge of a wood off the Mearns road. Over them was a sky of palest yellow stretching into the remote blue of the east, while above the distant city a dun streak from the setting sun penetrated the eternal roof of smoke. There was an activity in the silence around them of bird song and wind in the trees that was as an indefinite extension of the agitation in their breasts.

She opened the parcel hurriedly and paraded the contents on her knee with mock gravity. 'My word,' she said, 'that's fine!' Yet her gratification was more intense than she would willingly let him see.

'I'm going to put on the stockings now,' she decided, and

as she bared each foot he kissed it and begged that it remain
a moment uncovered. But she was eager to see the stockings
and how they would suit her, and she had her way.

'You are so thoughtful, darling—how ever can I tell you
how good you are!'

'I've only you to think about,' he replied.

'And I—I think of you every minute. I want only you. I feel
we should be away from all this—from everything we've ever
known, because our love is so unlike all—all the old things.'

It was of a lyrical sweetness to his mind. But as he did not
know how to sustain its beauty he took the words literally
and tried to make light of them.

'You'll soon forget that feeling. I have it too. But when we
get married you'll leave all the old things—never fear! We'll
be together all the time then except when I'm at the office.
Won't it be great! Think of you having tea ready for me in
our own home and waiting on me hurrying up the avenue
to be with you!'

She heard the word 'avenue' as she might notice a glint
of gold in dust. But it was all gold dust and she was covered
with it. Avenue. 'Hurrying up the avenue to be with you!'
So he meant them to stay there!

She became unaccountably sad. Or was it that the prospect
was so beautiful that the intervening days oppressed her?
He beseeched her to speak. What was it?

Tentatively she looked up and their eyes met. 'Elizabeth,
what of her?' she whispered. Would it not be cruel to leave
her? He laughed at her tenderness. 'You dear!' he said.
'Elizabeth has her own life to live. She'll be all right.'

They had never talked so frankly before and their words
gave them now, as dusk was descending, a greater need
of silence. Long afterwards, when daylight seemed like a
dream lost to the mind, they started from their quiet place,
over the dark fields and through breaks in the hedges and
over dykes until they reached the Eaglesham road, black and
smooth and starry, leading back to town. The little parcel

was under her arm, tucked away like a past experience whose interest was spent. Before them were the gathering lights of the city.

The Ringside Players were putting on the final show of the season three days before Easter, and David was invited to the first of the dress rehearsals. For company, and a little to satisfy his vanity, he asked Clifford to accompany him, and they took their seats with some other guests far back in the unlighted stalls. The club secretary came along and whispered that it would be a favour if the guests were to call out when the performers' voices fell too low or sounded otherwise ineffective. 'Don't be afraid to criticize us,' the secretary added, and it seemed that he meant what he said. Clifford, his hand at his mouth, whispered to David, 'If they've decent shanks it doesn't matter about their voices.' David nodded agreeably. 'After all,' he murmured, 'they're only amateurs.' To this Clifford assented blithely. He seemed to find something amusing in the word as applied to these players, and would have it that it was a comprehensive term. Yet with no discrimination he contrived to exclude Jessie from his bawdy joke. She was now reserved and apart. Her 'shanks' were not to be spoken of. Criticism would necessarily be concerned with her voice and histrionics, if indeed there was to be any criticism of her at all.

As the play proceeded, however, and Clifford's murmured commentary included references to all the other girls, these being his legitimate prey, his deference towards Jessie became as humiliating as his bawdy remarks could conceivably have been. It was a conscious restriction which had a worthless implication of fair play among friends. Instead of listening to the play, but allowing Clifford's asides to inflame his thoughts, David contemplated his position. He had fastened on to Jessie at the beginning to gain a measure of that experience upon which Clifford based his rights of superiority, and during his endeavours had been won over by her gentleness, her inherent decency, her simple expectation of his loyalty. Yet the terrible effect Clifford had on him in such a place as this was to make Jessie in common with the other girls on that stage look vulnerable to Clifford if not to him. Any one of them, confronted by him alone, could have stayed his unworthy purpose by a happy look or trusting word; but these would have been used by Clifford, subtly, pitilessly, to what might well be their actual biological conclusion.

His mind ached with an unclarified fear engendered by such thoughts, and an eerie feeling, experienced once before on a memorable night when walking home from Black Street, of having moved about in worlds not realized, took possession of him. But the memory of Jessie's gentleness and of her gladness in him was a resisting shield he had previously lacked and it aided him now when he turned suddenly with black venom on Clifford in those unlighted stalls. His lips parted snarlingly, to utter some ruthless disowning word, and though the word did not come Clifford moved back on his chair as upon some intuition of danger. When nothing happened Clifford whispered petulantly, 'What's up?'

He saw the angry ruffle on David's brow smooth away, as, pretending to be distracted, he leant forward, crooking his ear with his fingers interrogatively, 'Eh?'

'What's up?' Clifford insisted.

'Nothing. Why?'

'That's all right then. I thought you were peeved at something.'

'No, no.'

Clifford sat easy again, and David with a falling sickness within him looked once more at the stage where Jessie, having received some visitors of extravagant accent, was in the act of pouring tea from a silver pot. It was her own teapot, one of the 'props' the committee had elected her to supply, and she had asked David to look out for this significant scene. It would describe so much to him.

But the atmosphere was impossible. He could not endure Clifford's silence. Why hadn't he blasted him good and hard?

'I say,' he turned impetuously, 'let's go out for a drink— this is an uninteresting act.'

Clifford looked at him in amazement and then grinned brightly.

'A brilliant thought. Didn't think you had it in you.'

They excused themselves to others sitting near and tiptoed to an exit that was guarded by one of the theatre attendants.

'We'll be back shortly,' David whispered; 'we've got to phone a message home.'

The attendant nodded agreeably and they passed out.

'So this was what was in your mind,' Clifford guessed. 'Won't Jessie be hurt if she knows we went out?'

'I'll make some excuse. It doesn't matter.'

They hurried on in silence and in a few minutes were at a busy counter. 'What'll you have?' David asked.

'Beer. And so should you.' This had been David's idea, and it was therefore not incumbent on Clifford to be over-courteous. 'Remember what the ginger ale did to you.'

'Two beers, please,' David ordered without more ado.

The smell of beer, familiar to him for years, had fore-warned him of its taste, and now, when he took the first gulp, it seemed as though he was drinking a familiar smell. As on a former occasion, he copied Clifford closely, but at the same time he was amazed at his own past simplicity. This beer, which he had dreaded for years, was actually nasty, of a foul. repulsive nastiness such as would make it a thing of contempt for ever. The fear of danger died. He drank with the confidence of one who whips his hand unharmed through the flames of the fire for the entertainment of children. He would, he told himself, no more think of entering a pub to swallow this stuff by himself than a conjurer would hold his hand motionless amid the flames. The whole thing was a social trick.

Clifford grimaced, showing his teeth in the ecstasy of a quenched thirst that yet left him with a wersh taste in his mouth.

'Same again, old chap?'

David nodded, and the order was given.

'Why is it, Clifford, that you don't believe in people?'

'Don't believe how?'

'Well, in their virtue?'

'Never saw the need to.'

'I doubt that. What about your people, your mother?'

Clifford turned sharply, and David got a new impression of him as of someone consciously imitating a model.

'I don't think things like these should be discussed. You know nothing of my mother. She might have been an old harlot—'

'Clifford!'

'—In which case you'd probably have annoyed me. I'd have been sensitive. See?'

'I'll bet you would. But I didn't mean it that way.'

'I don't see what you're getting at anyway.'

'I just can't get used to the idea that everyone is what you think she is.'

'Don't, then.'

'Yet that's not it either. It's your attitude I don't understand or believe. You think it's a social fault when I show any sign of faith in women or show any sign of being decent myself.'

'Look here, David, either you're in this game or you aren't. It was the same when you came into a pub with me and drank ginger ale. You talk to me of women and yet you won't touch them. You want to know all I know and then start saying prudish things about me. You are too damned superior.'

'But that's the very point, Clifford, I'm not superior

and you don't believe I am. You despise me for social inexperience. You make immorality seem the sign of good breeding.'

'I don't care much for your terms. They're damned insulting.'

Again there came upon him that apprehensive uneasiness which his whole being challenged but could make nothing of. He was no longer angry nor did Clifford's words excite or vex him. Clifford would come round all right whenever he wanted him. Now he was concerned with something more deeply involving than Clifford's offended feelings. What was it? Was it this suggestion that his interest in women was as mean as the drinking of ginger ale in a pub? A year ago he wouldn't have understood what was meant. Today he knew perfectly well, and a vague foreboding as of the consequences of some forgotten foolishness swept over him.

People had this power upon him. Elizabeth, by assuming she knew of some irregularity about which she would not speak but which she disapproved, often left him baffled and unhappy, and only when his temper broke through and with an impatient shrug he tossed the whole subject from him could he climb out of the depths into which he had plunged. Thereafter he would muse on the strangeness of his experience, admitting that his mind had been on the point of discovering an important thing about himself and yet, on account of some slight inability, been thwarted.

Anger returned now as the subtleties of the situation still eluded him, and it was a defensive swagger of the spirit that at last obliterated the whole problem. His spirit rose against the too fine meanings and contempt of Clifford's world. What was that world worth anyway? It was all wrong and he was right. His natural disinclination for bawdy words and subterranean intrigues was the reaction of a healthy mind against something unclean. If Clifford's regard for women could stand comparison with the habit of drinking beer, then this beer he, David, had been drinking

was a taste of all Clifford had experienced, and it was foul
and debasing.

Without his usual 'Here's to luck to you,' Clifford had
already half-emptied his glass. David's stood before him
untouched. He now reached for it, marvelling that he could
be so emotionally excited while giving Clifford the impression of being still slightly depressed by their subject. He
judged as properly as he could the period of silence he had
enforced and made his rejoinder:

'There's one thing, Clifford; I'm not trying to insult you.
I'm only trying to find out about things.'

'Umph.'

'I lived a very sheltered life, you know, until I came to the
office.'

'It's wrong to hide behind the skirts of a woman straight
away.'

'You mean—?'

'I mean you should see life first before you get hitched up.'

'But you must mean your kind of life?'

'Less of that. Life.'

David nodded. 'Maybe.'

He finished his second glass, which he had found more
difficult, and almost immediately afterwards felt a slight
swerve within him upon which straight lines became ever
so delicately tilted. For the first time in his life he was
aware of his two eyes performing a single function. His
mechanical faculties were now by the very subtlest suggestion disharmonious. It was as though he had gripped the leash
of a phantom dog.

His capitulation had mollified Clifford, whose eyes cleared
once more. It was David's turn to suggest another drink, but
this did not occur to him. He was impatient to get back to
the rehearsal. They breasted the swing doors and made their
way to the theatre like men who, having been given the major
need of their manhood, were now prepared to countenance
the lesser joys of others.

But the excitement of this evening was only beginning. Things had been happening during their absence, and the first indication that something was wrong came to them when the man at the door spoke very differently from his previous pleasant manner.

'I'm letting no more people in here tonight,' he announced.

'But you remember us, surely? We've been out only a few minutes.'

'I don't remember nothin'. I've been told off for lettin' someones in alreadys, and I'm not doin' it any more without authority.'

'Well, get the secretary of the club. He'll tell you it's all right.'

The man agreed to this, and in a few seconds was back with the young fellow who had spoken to them in the stalls.

He was relieved to see David.

'We couldn't find you anywhere, and I didn't think to ask the doorman if you'd gone out. Miss Adair wants you.'

He led the way to the back and along a narrow corridor to the dressing-rooms. In one of these, alone beside a foul-smelling oil-stove, Jessie was sitting with her coat thrown loosely over her shoulders.

'Did you see him?' she asked, lifting heavy tear-filled eyes to David's face when Clifford and the secretary had retreated.

'See him?'

'Father. He's been here demanding the props I brought, and all because I took them when he said I wasn't to. He's given me a terrible time in front of everyone.'

'That's really dreadful,' said David. 'What happened?'

'He asked the secretary for the teapot and two cushions and a picture. And he's got them. I couldn't ever play now.'

'Don't be ridiculous. The club will understand.'

She covered her face with her hands, displaying her abject fear of the situation.

'See him, David,' she whispered, 'and tell him to go away.'

In the passage he found Clifford and the secretary leaning against the wall and smoking cigarettes. 'How's the tragedienne?' Clifford asked evenly.

'She's pretty seedy.' David turned to the secretary. 'Where is he?'

'He's in that room waiting for Jessie,' the young actor said, pointing to a door along the corridor.

David hurried along and found Mr Adair with his belongings arrayed on a table.

'Have you got everything?' he asked abruptly.

'All that I know of. How's Jessie?'

The eyes that turned on David were unbelievably mild.

'She's all right. I must say it was beastly of you to treat her like that among her friends.'

'I didna mean to do anything. She was told not to take the things out of the house. This playacting's all a cod anyway.'

'But you humiliated her among a lot of strangers. Why did you need to do that?'

Mr Adair's shoulders heaved, but his eyes remained as mild as a cow's. 'I dunno. She should have done as she was bid.'

David realized that the man had no notion of the cruelty of his act. This playacting was only a children's game which should not be allowed to subvert discipline. He had done no more than stumble into a kind of nursery.

'She'll be a' right, eh?' he queried.

'There's her mother, of course,' the man mumbled apart. 'She's better come away home.'

'I'll see that she gets home, Mr Adair.' David still spoke gruffly, but only out of loyalty to Jessie; he had no ill feeling left for the old man. 'You'd better go away before there's any more unpleasantness. I'll bring her home and the things with her.'

Mr Adair looked doubtfully at the silver pot. 'She's got a bag somewhere.'

'I'll get it. You had better go.'

David took him to the stage exit, where another theatre attendant was seated, and this man, who rose on David's signal, led Mr Adair to the door. 'Tell her no' to be long,' was his parting call, and David waved friendlily enough.

'See him off?' asked Clifford when David reached the passage once more.

'Yes; he's away.'

'Nice old chap he seems to be. Did he find his cushion— the one with the gold braid round it?'

'Give us a chance, Clifford; Jessie's upset.'

Clifford cocked an eye in such a friendly way that it was impossible to resent it. 'She'll be all right,' he said. 'And as I'll only be in the road I think I'll go. This excitement has made me thirsty.'

Infinitely relieved at his going, David went back to Jessie.

'Did you see him?' she whispered.

'Yes. He's gone home. You've to take the props.'

Her eyes were heavy with sorrow. 'Now you see what he's like.'

David nodded, but made no comment, and when a minute later she repeated with bitter emphasis, 'Now you see what he's like!' he had a remote feeling of shame.

'You are probably at cross purposes, Jessie,' he ventured.

She took this as a mere courtesy for which she had no use. 'We couldn't help but be,' she answered promptly. 'My whole life's at cross purposes with his and always will be, the beast!'

Again David was silent. Something in him resented her youthful bitterness. It was less convincing than the mild stupidity of the old man, about whose feeble words there had been a domestic and impersonal concern. It was an unimaginative and ugly thing that he had done, but it was not malicious or perverse. Jessie's anger rose from a hate that had always been in her; her words were ready and swift, for they had been learned long before this present affair.

As soon as they got the props into the bag they left the theatre. The show was going on with someone reading her part. But, though she could act no more that night and was visibly shaken, she would not go home. She was aware of the chance given her in this situation and was determined to use it to the uttermost. David's mind must be made fixed and unshakable in its impression of this parental cruelty. They crossed Sauchiehall Street and found their way to the darkness of Blythswood Square, at this time an oasis of quiet in the very heart of the city's night life. It had a small gravel pavement skirting a square of grass and shrubbery, and on this footpath they revolved interminably, talking things over. Slowly, and with a deepening emotion in her voice, Jessie showed that two roads only were open to her. She must either shift into lodgings, somewhere unbeknown to her father, or marry.

'He hates me and that's the truth,' she said passionately. 'It's no use deceiving you any more. He sneers at my acting and at my friends, at you, David, even. Says horrible things. He wants me to be a domestic slut, washing floors and stairs all my life. He can't see me sewing or knitting but he sneers. Think it's uppish and so on. It's horrible!'

He pressed her arm sympathetically, but was silent.

'I'm ashamed to tell you these things. You are so happy in your home affairs. You'll not understand.'

'I want to see you happy also, Jessie.'

'Well, take me away, anywhere—now!'

Her histrionic note kept the whole thing slightly tilted away from reality. He was aware that somewhere she laid an emphasis which distorted the truth, but for the life of him he could not discover where. Her nearness, on the other hand, in this surrendering mood, was making his heart race, so that in pretending to accept her tragic picture of herself he also was indulging in histrionics. It was an unreal situation she created for a private purpose of her own; and out of it, he saw, he might snatch something than which there is nothing more real in the world. Yet, on the moment of her impulsive gesture, when her hand climbed the lapel of his coat and her voice beseeched, 'Yes, yes, David, take me away tonight, now!' his mind rose above the temptation, even while he foresaw a future in which he might despise himself for this self-thwarting. He caressed her tenderly, and his voice said, 'Yes, darling, now, if you'd really have it so,' but immediately thereupon he removed her hand, interrupting very softly her impetuous gesture and by so much resisting the emotion behind it.

'You really cannot go on?' he asked, as though he would bring the whole thing back for review once again.

'No, not after tonight, David. I'm finished.'

They walked a few paces in silence.

'If you're certain there isn't any mistake . . . '

Hurt at this doubtful note, she turned away, impetuous still. He followed up quickly.

'No, no, dearest, I understand. It's just so tragic I keep hoping there might be a way out. But if you say no, then that ends it.'

'I just wish to be near you, David,' she said. 'You've taught me so much that's new. Probably that is why I can't stand him—any longer.'

Her voice had a strange richness in it, an appeal which isolated him from all the world and enchanted him. She infected him with her belief in his power and in his goodness so that he forgot her histrionics and responded as to an immediate presence of beauty. He caught at her hands, her soft and warm fingers, and drew her close. 'Don't worry, darling,' he said, 'I'll see that you are all right. You'll be away from it all soon.'

So that night when she lay in bed she knew she was going to get her chance. Her father and mother, asleep in the next room, were deserted in her mind as though she were bereaved of them. No thought of their pathetic position struck up a challenging counter to her plan. They simply did not count. For years past she had conceived of their generation as separated from hers by a dividing line as searing as death, more terrible than caste or race. Their natures fitted the habits they evolved, and to live with these habits forced upon her was as devastating as an association with Chinese or Africans, whose plan of living was utterly alien to her.

There was no hope of understanding, no possibility of contact. To be rid of them, to flee them, was her one and only hope of doing anything with her life. This solution to all her problems, after years of struggling with them, was ridiculously simple, yet she did not upbraid herself for not thinking of it sooner. She had had to go through with it. And, in any case, none of the other boys had the same romantic reliability. David was so negotiable.

She found him on their next meeting worried and unhappy. He was conscience-stricken for having allowed her to go home at all. Quickly judging her advantage in this development, but without stressing overmuch her embarrassment and humiliation, she encouraged his mood for action.

'It is really terrible,' she sighed, as though admitting the inevitable. Passion, it appeared, had died down, leaving her past regard for these people burned-out ashes. She sighed her decision in a manner that put David slightly in terror. Her calm had a deathly quietness. They walked down to a newspaper office and wrote out an advertisement for apartments.

Thereafter her mood brightened; she held closely to his arm and seemed to caper at his side like a gleeful child. In a little while she was coaxing him not to take her woes so seriously but to be bright with her.

'Think what fun it'll be, darling,' she said. 'I'll maybe get a place where you can come to in the evenings and we'll be all alone. I'll give you tea and entertain you! Won't it be great?'

He saw something lovely in that and his eyes cleared.

'And you won't regret leaving them—afterwards?'

'Huh! As if I would!'

'It's such a—a big thing to do.'

'Not when you know them.'

'Sure?'

'Positive.'

'Of course,' he reflected, 'you could always go back if you wanted and make some sort of explanation.'

'Catch me,' she pouted, and for a second the old unlovely smile hovered on her lips.

Two days later there were a shoal of responses to the advertisement. David collected them and went to see her direct from the office. There was one in Langside Road, just round the corner from Cornfoot Avenue, which was by far the most desirable, and of this he told her immediately. He was excited by it; the nearness and the niceness of the place and the moderate charges—was it not a new development of their romance, a working of a benign Providence? Once again she judged his mood acutely, allowing it to bear them both along its course. Her eyes were steely as they read the letter, her body taut and resolute. 'That's it,' she said. 'We must go out and see the woman right away.'

She was calm and quiet, he was excited and voluble. She let him talk, responding eagerly enough but never hiding a preoccupation with her own thoughts. It was as though she were sheathed in a fine steel. He probed her mood, to find her resilient and strong in resolve. The thing was actually happening: they were on their way out to see apartments where she might stay always and be alone. And as the tram trundled on, one of a hundred journeys it made that day, filled with unromantic-looking and uninspired people, she had David whispering at her side of the glorious times ahead.

'If we were married I'd be giving you all my salary. What difference is there, then, in my giving you a few bob every week? You're an orphan, really. I think we'll go and get married secretly so that I'll be able to give you money without hurting your silly scruples.'

She pressed his arm fondly. 'I'm game for anything,' she smiled.

'And I'll come to see you in the evenings,' he went on. 'You'll be sewing or knitting. Perhaps we'll read together. And you'll make supper. I'll know all about you then, where you sleep and what you do and the place that holds you. I'll be able to imagine you when I'm away. It'll make me so happy to know that you are comfortable.'

They visited the house and found conditions as suitable as they had dreamed. She was to have a large airy room from whose wide window she could see the trees and rising fields of Queen's Park. To the right was Cornfoot Avenue, the corner garden just showing beyond the gable-end of the tenement. Here she could sit in the summer evenings and have the rich green trees before her and the sunset skies. She would be able to see the people who entered Cornfoot Avenue and who came from it. She would be at that window to wave her greeting to him when he came for her and when he went away. It was so near, it was the next best thing to being together.

The woman of the house had sat under David's father for many years. She knew David much better than he knew her, having watched him on many a Sunday in the manse pew. To her the couple's arrival was as commercially attractive as she was romantic to them. Jessie, sensing the inherent respect for the minister's son in such a woman, assumed a lamblike docility. Her eyes were a melting softness as she looked from Mrs Watson to David and back to the elder woman again. She allowed David to do the talking. He was so keen to make everything just right. He told Mrs Watson that they were engaged, that she was an orphan, but had never been in lodgings before, and that of course, as she would find out, a good landlady was one in a million. Mrs Watson, who was ordinarily a cautious enough woman, knew that Providence had sent her a good thing and smiled unrestrainedly. Mr David needn't fret about his lass: she would be well looked after.

And so it came about that Jessie was definitely fixed to desert her home at the end of the week.

2

Though he was persuaded that this was the best thing to do and knew that his prospects would brighten a hundredfold by the decision, an uneasiness of the spirit never known before increased as the few remaining days went by. He was persuaded, yet in the hinterland of the mind there was a suspicion that Jessie had forced matters. He could not believe that Elizabeth in similar circumstances would have succumbed. Jessie's was a tacit acceptance of defeat, and defeat in this way meant a betrayal of duty, however repulsive and odious the circumstance.

The manner in which she proposed to leave home quickened his uneasiness. She intended to walk out of the house on Saturday morning and not go back. Her father would search the town and on Monday morning call at the shop. He would be afraid, however, to make a scene there, and she would tell him that she was not coming back. She would inevitably face up to him some time; but so long as it wasn't in the house, where he could corner and abuse her, she didn't care. There were some things she wanted desperately to tell him, and she would let him have these if he 'chased her up'.

This attitude seemed intolerably cruel in David's eyes. It was of the heartlessness of which she accused her parents. In maintaining it behind her bright smiles and gentle manner she seemed less justified in judging them. David at first asked incredulously, 'But can you let them worry a whole weekend, not knowing where you are?' and felt the inhumanity of her reply, 'It'll do them good,' as a personal assault.

Her expectancy that he would agree with this was a humiliation.

'Bad as they've been to you, Jessie, you needn't be cruel to them. You mustn't give them cause to revile you.'

'But I must leave. Why should I stand a first-class row if I can avoid it?'

'We'll have to think of something.'

Since the incident at the theatre and the prospect of sharing a responsibility of her actions developed, he had become almost masterful with her. There was a ring in his voice now that she respected and feared. But for the life of her she could not understand such scruples over people's feelings where hers had been so continuously outraged. She turned blankly to him, apprehensive yet interested.

'What can we think of? I've simply got to leave.'

'Are you leaving to hurt them or to escape?'

'I don't want to hurt them, of course, but I must escape or they will hurt me.'

I want you to go home tonight and tell them, simply, that you are going away.'

'Heavens! I couldn't!' She laughed grimly at the idea.

'Well, then, we must invent something. Go home tonight and tell them you've got a new job with a bigger salary somewhere—somewhere out of Glasgow.' The idea formed rapidly in his mind. 'You can say Dundee. That's too far for your father to visit you and too expensive for you to visit them. Tell them you've been sacked from your present place and must take the new job.'

'They'll never believe it,' was her first thought, but as she considered it she saw the advantages to be gained. Such a story would indeed let her get away in peace and save any

subsequent unpleasantness. It would also enable her to
gather her belongings together openly. She might secure a
few extra things her mother was willing to give.

'All right, then,' she decided, 'I'll do that. And we shan't
be bothered with them afterwards.'

On Saturday afternoon David was waiting at the corner
of Dumbarton Road. Never had he waited on her with such
wavering and interweaving of feeling, such anxiety, such
expectancy. For Jessie was coming to him on the start of
a new life where she would be under his protection. It was
the beginning of bridal days, to end in their wedding. The
excitement of the event recalled the start of holidays long
ago, when he waited on Elizabeth and Jane at the railway
station and the notice for the train to Oban was posted on the
big black information-board. But it was more exciting than
that. Jessie would come to him from that sordid house like
someone turning her face to the light.

It was a beautiful April day and its spring freshness
added subtly to his agitation. The sun, unseen behind tall
buildings, flooded Dumbarton Road with a tender amber
light. Shop windows were panes of gold and high warehouse
and tenement windows sparkled like diamonds beside others
whose angles caught the mild blue of the sky and missed the
slanting sun. The people passing David seemed unaware
of the beauty around them and untouched by the spring,
just as months ago he had seen people remote-looking and
uninfluenced by signs of Christmas in the city streets. But
when Jessie came along and stepped out of the passing
stream to gaze excitedly into his face, his eyes, concentrated
on her alone, found hints of the spring about her that his
casual glance might well have missed in others. She wore a
fawn-coloured smooth-faced coat with a collar embroidered
with green and red roses stitched around with gold, and a
girdle of the same colours hung negligently from clasps at
her side. The coat had one enormous button upon which
the poise of the garment depended, and it was fastened by a

clasp of red and green.

Those little red and green roses, with their little rim of gold, how distracting they were! And on her hat, repeated in cunning undertones, little gold roses, lined by green and red! And her face under the hat, radiant with new-found happiness.

She had been carrying two commodious-looking bags, which now rested at her feet. For a minute in that jostling thoroughfare they stood with only a breathless exclamation of greeting passed. They would not meet on their wedding-day with such unpremeditated joy.

'I'm away,' she breathed.

'And everything all right?'

'Yes.'

David cast a fleeting glance round. 'Sure he's not about, watching—suspicious?'

'Oh no. He's safe at home.'

'Then it's us for Langside Road. Come on.' He grabbed both bags and they hurried to a tram stop. The sun was bright on their faces, and even in that congested area, where smoke seems ever a roof above the head, the air was wine-sweet and intoxicating with the spring.

Mrs Watson had expected that he would be with Jessie and she had tea set for two. But before they could sit down there were a hundred and one things to do. He helped Jessie to unpack the bags, and was called on time and again to decide some detail in the displacement of the room. A wardrobe stood beside the bed, rather awkwardly placed for the eye, but convenient, and his verdict generally was towards this commodious if ugly piece of furniture. Into it at the start disappeared the fawn coat with the red and green roses and the tricky little hat, but soon the rods were loaded with dresses and frocks, blouses and skirts, all beautifully ironed, and some, it seemed, absolutely new. David looked and wondered. There was something in the presence of these new garments not calculated on and certainly unexplained in their scheme. How came she by them?

With a sickening of the spirit he answered this for himself. She had got them from her parents, who had made an effort to start her off well in her new life. She would not say so and he would not ask, yet so it was most patently, and her callousness dismayed him. Could her parents, he asked himself, be the insufferable creatures she had described, when they responded thus liberally to their sense of duty? And how, knowing that she was on the point of betraying them, could Jessie have accepted these clothes? These things his reason pondered, but beside them there was another thing. She had so trained him to despise her parents and to regard himself as her sole friend that he could not help viewing these new possessions with a jealous disappointment.

But he was growing skilled in silent observation, and his eyes remained sunny and unquestioning while she, escaping as she thought the possible embarrassment of an explanation, decided that in any case the matter was not worth while explaining. There was this chance, that he had not noticed, and it was a chance to be accepted. At tea, when finally it was brought in, they sat at the little table at the sun-filled window and she prattled like a child, with gleeful airs and unclouded eyes.

She had nothing more truthful in her to tell him than that this was the fulfilment of the first part of her dream and that the rest was ever so much more likely now. There was nothing to come between them, nothing to alienate him, nothing to nauseate him so that he might lose his boyish ideas of her. From the optimism of this sprang her rapid glowing words in which she made her voluntary covenant to live for and think of him only. He listened and slowly his uneasiness died away. She was for him only: eager, impetuous, truthful, wanting to be with him alone. Such utter abandonment would not have happened had her people been decent as he was. Suppose she were guilty of exaggeration in her enmity with them, was it not partially the result of seeing them more clearly now, with the clearness of the eyes of love? We want to be like those we love and those who would hinder us we hate.

'. . . But it will be nicer than this when we are married,' she was saying, and they looked round the room. It had grey walls with a brown border and a dingy enough ceiling. A broad sofa in green velvet stood back from the window, and several chairs of the same material, but badly worn, stood at odd intervals against other walls. The carpet was brown, showing a tiny path threadbare from the door. On the walls were heavily framed portraits of unknown people and on the overmantel were smaller frames with similar subjects. Yes, certainly it would be nicer when they were married. But lodgings were always the same, and inevitably one didn't know the photographed friends of the landlady. All that mattered meantime was the cleanliness of the place and the food. For the place was a haven in which she was merely waiting.

'You'll remember this place afterwards,' he speculated, 'and maybe love its memory.'

'Oh, I love it now,' she cried happily. 'It's wonderful. But what I mean is, it's not ours.'

It was always this way. She returned again and again to the thought of them together. Nothing else mattered and for the beauty of that hope she was prepared to endure and to sacrifice anything.

Well, if the present did not matter, why had she left her home? But that was different. She had not been enduring the evils of home—which he knew nothing of—for him; there she had suffered needlessly and endlessly. Now, in a room in a strange house, she was prepared to live alone and concentrate upon passing interests of a perishable nature until she could come to the permanence of his home. She was there, waiting for him.

How subtly this worked upon his mind when he was
with her! The prompting of his love was to accept it and
to be jubilant over it and honoured by it. Any doubting of
her action in leaving her parents was a slight to their love, a
wanton darkening of their sky.

But however often her enthusiasm swept him up and his
heart quickened at her fondness, however deeply stirred he
was by the sight of her happiness, the changed look in her
eyes at parting, the calm clear look at meeting, he was fated
to torture himself with questionings. His sense of home had
been violated, and his mind went speeding back in silent
hours to the memories of old days when home was sacred
and permanent-seeming as life itself. And inevitably in the
long run he betrayed his doubts. They were revealed to
her by flashes which were quickly shut off by energetic
assurances of his trust in her. She saw them and was
perplexed and angered. But each time she yielded to the
assurances and smiled again, just as he was giving way to
her charms and forcing himself to believe that he believed
in her.

A fortnight passed and their life had ordered itself into
a routine which pleased them well. They were continuously
together, in town or country or sitting in her room. Mrs
Watson 'encouraged' him to come. It was so much better
that he should be with her in the room than that they
should be walking about outside. David brought fruit and
chocolates and pastries, which went into the kitchen and of
which Jessie got an adequate share. Mrs Watson, remembering the minister, thought David a worthy son. All seemed
set for a happy summer could David but surrender himself
entirely to it.

This, however, he was unable to do. The mind that is
questing in doubt knows no rest. David's persistence in
pondering her position was more intense than his desire
to enjoy her company. And so in time he came upon
a new fear, such as his doubt was bound ultimately to

throw up, and this had to be put to Jessie. She would hate him for bringing it up, but it had to be. One evening when they were lying on the edge of a wood near Cathcart Castle, he began:

'They are getting no letters from you. What will they think? There's sure to be a time when they'll be suspicious. And then, what will they do? Don't you see the danger? Your father will probably call at your shop to get the address of the new place in Dundee. Then there will be a row.'

'Well, David, it's your fault, really. We'd have been far better to tell them plainly what we were doing.'

'You refused to do that.'

'I'd have done it when I met him afterwards.'

'Could you?'

'Couldn't I just! And I will, if he comes to the shop.'

Almost timidly he asked her, once again, 'But are both of them, your mother as well as him, utterly indifferent? Do they hate you?'

'Utterly. Gracious! You surely saw for yourself.'

That was the difficulty: he had not seen it for himself. Indeed, the vague disturbing indications had been that it was not so. But she was showing an ability in such passages of making him appear insensitive and coarse, and already her chin was up and there was a haughty look in her eyes. He hurried to placate her. Yet in his soothing words he was speaking to the unspoken in her.

'Some people might think you had been heartless, Jessie, but that's a danger you don't need to mind. After all, *we* know you'd never have left them had they had a spark of affection for you.'

'But even if they did care for me a little, Father's treatment was too awful. Ugh! he couldn't have cared and carried on as he did.'

For a second it seemed she had admitted the possibility and had then shuddered back upon her old prejudices. He glanced at her swiftly as the phrase 'even if they did care for me a little' was locking his doubts securely in his heart. There was defiance in her attitude which was in subtle conflict with the honest disgust of her words. But as he looked she turned, her troubled expression disappearing as she smiled, her hand reaching out for his. They clasped and said no more.

The common words and phrases of every day were instinct with deeper meaning when she used them. He was for ever finding some subtle interpretation of her blossoming in his mind long after she had spoken. It was a process of revelation of character, both by words and voice, a revelation that was inevitable no matter how hard she strove to maintain the conception she wished. His divinating cunning got through the false to her true self.

'Even if they did care'. It was a premise she had allowed only to cancel it in a wave of revulsion. The idea, she showed, was preposterous. But, clever as she was, the truth had been revealed in it.

He did not wish to believe this, God knew. He wanted her for himself, her kisses and embraces, her whispered secrets of her womanhood, her passion and desire for him. She was without encumbrances now: every moment of her leisure was his. It was surely to his advantage to believe that she had been justified in running away to be near him. But, if she had not been true in this, how could she be trusted otherwise? He had to prove one thing or the other; and the method he chose was decided upon quite suddenly one early evening when the sight of a red tramcar in Argyle Street put him in mind of Black Street. Why not go out there and see with his own eyes the conditions from which Jessie had fled?

It was a bold move and one which Jessie would have thought treacherous to a degree. But if it vindicated her he would know and he would come away and never, never doubt her again.

He went with no formulated plan, depending on his wits to see him through. It was an adventure lined with a romance of his own past, for during the months he had known Jessie in Black Street, drab and slightly odorous as it was, the place had been touched with the glamour of the mystery of her. Entering her home at long last, he would break that spell; and the anticipation of it sent a faint tingling to the fingertips.

It was barely six o'clock when he arrived, and he interrupted Mr Adair, who, with his jacket off and sleeves rolled up, was in the act of washing the kitchen floor. The old man led him into the kitchen, and they faced each other over the wet line on the worn linoleum where his operations had ceased. Beside them stood a pail of soapy water. A kettle was steaming quietly on a gas-ring at the hearth-side, and under the ring there were a couple of chops on a slowly sizzling grill-pan.

'Ay, I'm busy the now. You've got me at a bad time.'

'I'm sorry disturbing you, then,' David replied, 'but I just dropped in to say I was going to Dundee tomorrow on business and will probably be seeing Jessie. I thought you might have some message for her.'

'Dundee, eh?' the father replied, without enthusiasm. He seemed more taken up with the washcloth he held in his hands. 'Aye, she hasna sent us any word. We hav'na even her address.'

'Neither have I,' David said in his shame. Then he pulled himself up, floundering, 'But I'll find her.'

'It'll no be easy; Dundee's no village. Of course, I hav'na been there for a long time.' Mr Adair bent down to the pail and rinsed the cloth in the soapy water.

'No, but I think I know the shop.' David spoke to the back of the man's head. Then, with a touch of desperation, 'I'm sure to find her.'

'Ay? We don't even know the shop.'

'It's thoughtless of her. She should have written you.'

'I daresay. Her mother's bothering aboot it.' The man's voice was no more than a murmur. 'The wife's bedridden, you see. She's naethin' to do but fret. They didna get on well thegither.'

'I'm so sorry. I didn't know.'

Mr Adair looked up slowly, making a show of his calm. There was no need to extend sympathy to him. Then his shoulders quivered slightly and he went on as though finishing his sentence:

'But it doesna worry me.'

Here was a brief wearied criticism of the whole affair. But, brutal as it sounded, David could not get it to sort with the tales Jessie had brought of his bitterness and indifference. It was not a characteristic indifference, but a disposition developed through the years.

The man looked clownish. David caught an aspect of him that was in the very spirit of fun; his bauchly legs, wet knees, dirt-smeared sweaty face, his fingers fondling a washing-cloth; but over all there was a sense more powerful which saved him from the ridiculous and swayed David into confusion. He was dejectedly bored. One cannot smile inwardly at a man, howsoever comical he appears, if his boredom dominates the situation.

'Well,' said David hesitantly, 'I just wondered if I could be of any service to you. I'll be going now.'

Their eyes met and David tried to catch hold of his gaze and support it as one seizes a staggering man; but it was no good. The gaze wavered and fell, slipping off with a touch of interest in David's shoes. It was meanly, covertly contemptuous. 'The man thinks I'm a weed,' thought the boy.

'You had better see the wife when you are here. I'll tell her.' He let the washcloth fall with a flop into the bucket and crossed to the door. A nod invited David to follow.

The bedroom where the woman lay was long and narrow like a coffin and indescribably untidy. Two trays of dirty dishes lay on the floor beside the bed. A plate of scones, evidently forgotten, was at the back, half covered with tossed-up blankets. Clothes of every description lay heaped on chairs, on the floor, thrown over the foot of the bed and dumped against the side of a tall wardrobe. The room's single window, shaded by a long draggled lace curtain, was dim with dirt.

'Here's a freen of Jessie's who's goin' to Dundee the morn,' said Mr Adair to the bed. 'He's come to see if you've any message for her.'

He stopped and lifted one of the trays. 'I hav'na had time to clean up here yet,' he murmured.

David looked at the woman in the bed and a hush came over his heart. A white face lay on the soiled pillow, lay perfectly still, and only the eyes, remarkably alert, dark brown and glowing, acknowledged his greeting. They fastened on his face greedily, and in a moment he was endeavouring to beat them down, but as vainly as, some minutes ago, he had tried to steady the man's. Mr Adair with the tray passed out and left them alone.

'Are you her latest?' The voice was startlingly loud.

He smiled wanly, fighting down a sickness in his heart. Whatever expression she saw on his face, he thought, it would damn him.

'I don't quite know what you mean,' he said mildly. 'I'm a friend of Jessie's and I may see her in Dundee tomorrow. I shan't be there long. Only a few hours. But I thought you might have something for her—some message—that I could take. That's all.'

'Shan't be there long?' Her eyes were fixed now.

'No,' he nodded.

'You're not keeping her somewhere, are you?'

The question came on him like a blow. He seemed thrown clear of her gaze and his eyes shifted to the hulk of her under the clothes. He felt his risen blood stain his cheeks. In a desperate effort at scorn he replied, 'I did not come here to be insulted,' and caught at the door.

But the brown eyes were squirming their way back. It was as though he were being held by an iron hand.

'Why doesn't she write?'

'I don't know,' he snapped. 'She hasn't written to me.'

'Are you her young man?'

'—No. I'm just a friend.'

'What do you expect to get, being just a friend?'

'This is too bad. I really must be going.'

'A minute. Why did you come? What did you say?'

'I thought I might have the pleasure of taking Jessie a surprise. That's why I came. I am disappointed. But you must hate Jessie if this is the way you talk of her. She's better away from you.'

For the first time the fierce clutching look in the eyes weakened. Yet the gaze relaxed nothing.

'Why doesn't she write!' It was a high querulous voice now, repeating this less as a question than as an exclamation.

He stood irresolute. Then once again he relented, he scarcely knew why.

'Perhaps she is not good at writing.'

'I can't write even though she sent her address. I'm paralysed. But her father can. Her father is a good writer.'

With this the storm had gone out of her voice. But it was still loud in David's ears like a strong wind blowing after the yell of a gale. He looked at her pityingly.

'It must be wretched for you to lie here and get no letters. When one has nothing to do one worries over anything.'

The head nodded ever so slightly and a look of yearning came into the eyes. There was something fluid and slimy now in their contact with his. The clutching had stopped.

'You will be missing her company—she must have been a big help to you in the house?'

How quickly the situation had been transformed! He was seated again and putting a question to her. And it was such a question as now, after the rebuke he had given her, and those adroit touches of conciliation he had shown, she dared not answer. The whole thing was as plain as the palm of his hand. She dared not risk the answer she was longing to give.

It seemed then that the exercise of restraint paralysed her tongue. Her eyes burning within their hollows in the white face had the paralysed answer floating in them. And of this she seemed pitiably conscious.

'Well,' he started, as though his question had been a mere statement of fact settling their talk, 'will I take anything to her? Have you a message for her?'

'Tell her to write. Say I'm just the same. But tell her to write.'

'I will. And I hope you won't worry. I'm sure she's all right. Can I come back and tell you about her?'

The eyes clutched again. 'I'm lonely here. I'd like you to come back. But tell her to write. There'd be an address then and a postage-mark to look at.'

His heart hardened again, for this showed that he had made no impression at all. She had no right to be suspicious. It was only a chance that. . . . She might easily have been all wrong.

'Does that mean that you don't believe Jessie is in Dundee? If so, I'd rather not come back to see you.'

The look in her eyes faltered, and then, for the first time, came tears. 'You're not lying here,' she wept in excuse. 'If you were lying here you'd be glad to know that everything was all right.'

He sighed. 'I'm sorry. I don't mean to hurt you.'

'You'll tell her to write and you'll come back soon?'

'Yes.'

'How soon?'

'Well, perhaps Wednesday?'

'That's the day after tomorrow? All right.'

'Goodbye.'

The eyes gave him release. 'Goodbye,' she said, and turned her face to the wall.

In the dark lobby, where by this time there was a smell of grilled chops, Mr Adair appeared from the kitchen. He came holding a fork, still in his shirtsleeves and still wet about the knees. As he opened the front door and David strode forward he murmured, nodding his head at the bedroom, 'Paralysed.'

'Yes,' David replied, 'she told me. It's a dreadful disease.'

'Fourteen years since, come June,' the low voice went on. David was on the doorstep.

'So long ago?' he said concernedly; but feeling the door coming at him he kept moving out; and when his foot was clear of the step it shut with a snap.

This was his memory when that same evening Jessie and he were once more on the edge of the wood beside Cathcart Castle. They were sitting on a fallen tree-trunk near the spot where an ancient stone was alleged to mark where Mary Queen of Scots stood searching the valley below with eager eyes on the day of the battle of Langside. The castle midway down the hill stood out of the dim darkness, a black hulk among the springtime trees. Near hand there was the tinkling of timid water.

Glasgow lay before them, a great sweep of tiny points of light. The nearest of these, the lamps of Cathcart railway station, outlined a familiar shape, and farther off the constellation of lights within a factory by the river Cart loomed among the lesser lights of tenement buildings like a ship lit up in the docks. All was quiet around them. Jessie's head was resting on his shoulder in a deep content.

'I met your father today,' David told her innocently.

'Heavens, where?'

'In town. He recognized me, I'm surprised to say. He asked me if I had heard from you. I said no. It was a rotten position to be in.'

'My poor angel, how dreadful!' She put her arm round him with a protective flourish, repeating 'dreadful!' in a whisper.

'Yes, darling, rather dreadful,' he owned, sitting quite still. 'But your position is rather bad. You see, they're naturally expecting word from you. He asked why you hadn't written, and I said you hadn't written me. But that was no excuse. I said I was going through to Dundee tomorrow on business and would likely see you. He asked me to call and tell them how you were.'

'Father did?' She clipped this at him, and both her manner and her words were all-important to him.

'Yes,' he replied boldly, listening.

She accepted it, but her surprise was real. 'Umm. Father's coming on.'

She meant that such social energy was unusual in him.

'He said your mother was worrying.'

'She would!' came with that some clipping smartness.

'I promised,' he continued evenly, 'to go and see them on Wednesday.'

'David, darling, what on earth for?'

'Could I refuse?'

She withdrew her arm and caught at her knees in a crouching attitude.

'But, darling, I *left* them, didn't I?'

'Nevertheless, if they are anxious it would be inhuman to keep silence.'

'But what good will your going do?'

'I don't know about that. I can tell them that you are getting along all right and that you have promised to write.'

'But I can't write from Dundee, can I?' she exploded.

'Why, yes, you can. Now, listen, dear, tomorrow you'll write a letter and give it to me and I'll take it to them. Then on Saturday, your half-day, you can catch the one-fifteen train from Glasgow, and you'll reach Dundee shortly after three. You can have a letter ready, and all you need to do is to post it there and come back.'

'That's going to be expensive. And then—the address?'

'Oh, invent something. Say you are shifting your lodgings next week and will write again when you are fixed. Anything at all. That'll give us time to think out some plan.'

'But why two letters? Surely if we post the Dundee one on Saturday, that will be enough?'

He thought about that. Then he nodded, 'All right, one will do meantime.'

'Umm.'

'Perhaps in a fortnight's time you can write again and say you are coming to Glasgow for a day and will be to see them. No need for an address even then. And so it could go on.'

She was silent.

'What do you say to that?'

'I'll do anything you like, David,' she murmured. Her head sank once more on his shoulder and there was a tearful note in her voice as she went on, 'But I thought I was to be free now and happy at last!'

'But, Jessie, if they are worried—'

Her voice soared impatiently. 'You don't know what you are talking about. You can't know!'

There followed then a period of quiet during which they both searched in the aura that, despite their bravest efforts, surrounded them separately. She was filled with fear. There came to her the signal of danger in the very elaboration of his plan to keep her free of danger.

'You shouldn't bother going on Wednesday. You'll only be insulted. It will make me so miserable.'

This was whispered with her lips against his cheek. But he did not answer. The words did not seem to matter: he was listening to something more intense that was of the spirit behind them. For there he sensed something deeper than the words ordinarily conveyed, the caressing tone of her voice being a physical interpretation for the imagination. His body suddenly glowed in the reception of a promise at which her conduct had hinted since coming to Langside Road.

She was close to him, her eyes dreamily gazing into the shadows and blackness of the wood beyond. And her whisper, when she began again, was soft as the velvety dusk.

'Darling, let us wait till Saturday and we can both go through to Dundee. I'll write the letter. And we don't need to be back until Sunday night.'

Apprehended though it had been, the vividness of her words raised him into the full enchantment of her meaning. She had a mother's tenderness in her caresses, protective, possessive. His mind emptied of everything for the moment save desire for her and a blind belief that such love as this must bring about an orderly life in which she would be as greatly admired as she was now desired.

The moon was high above Queen's Park when he left her at the close in Langside Road and turned into Cornfoot Avenue. Its starkness in the empty sky worked a subtle terror into the silence of the night. When a ship boomed far off on the Clyde he quickened his pace and felt grateful for the shattering of the silver silence. But it flowed into him and swept round him swiftly again. All Glasgow was battened down for the night, resting. And the moon shone down indifferently as though Glasgow's stretch were a sheet of meadowland. But the quietness was not the quietness of night upon a meadowland. It was only a lull, a hesitation between hammer-blows in an eternal workshop. That booming ship was a hint of the illusion of this silvery stillness. That was why the moon, sailing as though she were sailing over a Glasgow meadowland, struck terror into a silence that was arranged and not endowed. The vision of a paralysed body lying in a narrow coffin-like room was as flimsy as moon-rime on shrubs in the gardens. But it was real: she existed away over there under the moon-blanched roofs of Partick. Cunning as he thought himself to be, and eager at heart to be fair and wise, he could get little from the memory of that figure of the significance of pain. Not in that moonlight and straight from the kisses of one who, to be near him, had fled from the too close reality of that spectral creature, 'bedridden', as it was called, 'fourteen years since', according to the man.

The moon quenched the street-lamp's reflection upon his bedroom wall. When he got into bed he lay comforting his limbs in the cool sheets and looking at the silver in the room. 'Bedridden' was she, poor paralysed woman! Her dark eyes glowed in the mind. He lay contemplating them for a time, and then his thought roamed over the prospect of Dundee at the week-end.

But those dark eyes were glowing in the mind. They were living eyes and they could record living thoughts and change with a change of pain. They were no vision, but a challenge, direct and fierce. The girl, taking fright at the thought of him getting to know too much, was trying to distract and waylay him in the inevitable fashion. Those eyes had no terror for her. She who had known their influence for years had fled them unaffected. It was on him, with his memories of another spectral figure, that the challenge fell.

There had been some preparations for his visit on the Wednesday. Mr Adair was again without his jacket and his sleeves were rolled up, but he did not appear to be employed. The house had a cleaner air, a fresher look.

He was taken at once to the bedroom. The removal of loose clothes he had seen lying about and the tightening of the lace curtain at the window, with a few other deft touches, had transformed the place. It had width and a feeling of airiness. The woman in the bed seemed to have dwindled in the ampler space around her.

But the clutching look was back in her eyes and the initial uneasiness of guilt crept back into his. Two days had passed and she had struggled free of the softening influence of his reassuring voice; she was once more venomously suspicious. The orderliness of the room, however, and other signs of their preparedness told him that the impression he had left behind had not been entirely lost. Behind all this display of unbelief in her attitude there was a desire to believe. Getting the feel of this he faced the clutching eyes resolutely.

'It has been a sunny day,' she said.

'Yes.'

'You can have a chair. Mr Adair'll sit on the bed.'

The chair the man pointed to as he sat down heavily on the bed's edge stood off from the door and was positioned so that when David sat down the light from the window was full on his face. He felt that even this had been arranged.

'You would see Jessie?' the voice rapped out.

'Yes, I saw her. But only for a few minutes.'

'What did you say your name was?'

'David Carruthers. Sorry. I ought to have told you—'

'Did she give you her address?'

'No, by the way, she didn't. She said she was staying somewhere in Auldhouse Drive. But she's flitting at the week-end and she's promised to send on her new address.'

The woman's lips narrowed.

'Why should she send the new one when she's never sent the old one?'

'Well, for one thing, because I made her promise. And I think she really wants to write. She seems lonely.'

'She'll not be lonely long.'

'What do you mean?' he asked sweetly, temperately.

But the woman regretted the slip as soon as it was made. She pressed on with her list of questions, which apparently she had by rote.

'What's the name of the shop?'

'Marshall's, isn't it?'

'I don't know.'

'Yes.' (Was he losing ground?)

'What street's it in?'

'I'm sure of that. It is in Commercial Road,' he replied blithely. 'It's the big shop at the corner of—'

'I don't know Dundee.'

'It's a wheen years since I was there myself,' interposed Mr Adair.

'She promised to write to you,' David said. 'She would have written, but she wasn't in the mood, she said. She's been miserably lonely and seemed distressed when she spoke of you.'

'Distressed? What was she distressed about?'

'She was secretive and wouldn't say.' He stopped. It was impudently vague, this talk of his, and somehow, though it had succeeded on Monday, he could not make it convincing now. Feeling his security threatened, he had no compunction in tightening the screw. 'Tell me, if I may ask, why did she go to Dundee?'

'There was supposed to be better money in't,' Mr Adair murmured, and then, with a slight rise of his voice, 'least, that's what she said.'

David, still looking at the eyes in the bed, nodded.

'Was that it? Or was she not happy in Glasgow?'

It was a cruel challenge to those eyes burning in their selfish preoccupation. Here was the alertness and savage defiance of a mother beast at bay with her young. The litheness and sinuosity of limbs were incalculably trans- ferred to those searching, resisting, steadfast eyes. Behind them lay her own private thoughts upon her daughter, and these she guarded from this intruder until she knew more about him. He might be, he quite possibly was, a saviour, in which case he was never to know these thoughts. But, if she found him out a waster, then her hate would blaze on him and her thoughts accuse him with incrimination: then she would tell him all he wanted to know and he would go away, his purpose achieved. This he knew, and his instinct was to act upon it in self-defence. But the instinct was curbed by deeper feelings aroused by the humanity which shone through the woman's selfishness. For her the moment might have staked her life.

'I wonder!'

It was a quick sigh from her, suspending decision, and David's intuition worked upon it. What did she mean? Was it of him she wondered only, or of his question, suggested, as it might have been by Jessie, in unknown ways? Was it of the reality of his visit, or of her own suspicions?

Blindly David spoke again.

'She certainly seemed unhappy.'

Mr Adair, who also had hesitated on a rejoinder, now stirred himself on the bed's edge and met David's emphasis with a murmur:

'Perhaps she doesn't like lodgings.'

'But I mean, was she not unhappy in Glasgow?'

Silence.

As though absorbed by his own thoughts, David continued, 'I don't like to think of her in a strange town. She's too—she's of a highly nervous temperament—'

As he spoke he saw the woman in the bed accept her release as a torturer must see the change on relaxing a thumbscrew. The tone of his voice had told her he was not waiting an answer. She need say nothing now.

'—And that's why I wondered at her going away from home where she was sure of love and guidance.'

'Are you seeing her again?'

'Yes, I expect so. She said she'd be in Glasgow soon, and was, of course, coming to see you. But I might see her also.'

'That will be nice.'

So. By this it was evident she believed in him. He was in love with Jessie and, by a miraculous chance, he was decent. Therefore the truth of Jessie's departure as she conceived it had to be kept from him.

He let her keep her view. But she couldn't deceive him. He had known all along why she stopped dead at any answer of importance. The moment he had found Mr Adair washing the kitchen floor he had understood—everything. Why did he not face it and say to the woman, 'I know what you are hiding from me. The girl has forsaken you when you need her most. She tired of washing floors and so on. She tired of you and the duty you imposed.' He turned with a savage look at the man. Unless the trouble was really here! But all that was against the man was a lack of savvy in social manners, a lack of interest, a lack of money. His manhood debased by years of hardship and ill health, he was now content to go dithering about in his shirtsleeves, washing floors and cooking chops.

'She sends her love to you, anyway,' David told them as his eyes became calm and he smiled again. 'She says she's sewing something for you. She spends all her time sewing.'

'Ah God!' the woman's voice trembled.

'What is it?'

Her face was suddenly distorted with pain. Mr Adair rose and motioned David toward the door. 'She has turns,' he said, simply.

'I am sorry. Should I go?'

The man shut his lips approvingly.

'I hope I haven't excited you, Mrs Adair,' David whispered over her husband's shoulder. 'I will come and see you soon again.'

'Yes, come again soon,' came from her thin blue lips.

Mr Adair followed him into the lobby. 'Ay, so long,' he nodded, ignoring an offer to shake hands as he went forward to the door. David had never heard anything more hollow than that voice sounding from the depths of boredom.

It occurred to him as he walked down Byars Road and round the side of the Western Infirmary, that perhaps he should have taken a small present to that house, a cake or a flower or two. He searched his pockets and, finding a private card, went into a florist's where he chose some beautiful white and red tulips to be sent forthwith. That would give her his address. It was a voluntary action, and yet as he continued on his way he felt he had executed something planned long ago and waiting to be done.

Extending her power over him by giving her his address, however, would complicate matters. It was another of those little actions of self-thwarting he was so good at. It was so nice, so proper, so above-board. It hinted that there was no possibility of his doing anything the little paralysed woman would condemn. This idea of Jessie's, of going to Dundee for the week-end, for instance.

Jessie's whispered words, 'We need not come back till Sunday night,' had played the devil in his mind while in that sick-room. For in the presence of the mother they became something tangible which he had stolen from her, a portion of herself that was still sweet and unparalysed. Now that he was alone in the pleasantly sunlit street, however, he could think of the enchanting whisper as one might take out a stolen jewel and gloat upon it.

Jessie had lied to him, lied and most cruelly misrepresented. He had spied on her and found her out. Yet could he, of all the world, blame her? She had wearied of the incessant drudgery in that house and of the hopelessness of its outlook. And she had wanted to be near him, to be near and to be free, continually free to come to him. It was out of desire for him that she had left; otherwise, would she not have gone away years ago? Desire for him, and a secret fear that the house would shame her in his eyes if he were taken to it.

His spying visits had brought all this to light; and she, sensing danger, had surrendered with 'We need not come home till Sunday night.' He felt himself like some hooded judge standing apart and watching.

What would he do? What was to become of her? He could not marry her now. Yet he would not let her go. He was worse than Clifford, who always showed his shallow meaning. There was no depth in Clifford like this in which he was seeing his past convictions, his inherited principles drowning. For to go with her to Dundee now was a hundred times worse than to have seduced her at the beginning as was his secret thought. That beginning seemed almost boyish and pure to him now. He had known nothing of her then; she was merely a girl. Now she was Jessie, the unparalysed, sweet and healthful part of that stricken wonderful woman high up in a Partick tenement.

What could he do with her? Send her back? She would not go. He would not let her go. Not like that. But if they went to Dundee he could make a great show of sorrow afterwards, a sort of mental wringing of hands. And, being superstitious about premature fulfilment, she might believe that it had altered his love for her. It would make him the guilty one and give her the appearance of virtue by being wronged. She'd storm and she'd weep; but she would ultimately realize the futility of protest where love was killed. Then, in a reaction against him, she might go back to her mother.

That was a scheme worthy a bawdy grin from Clifford. But the mind that could devise it could despise it at the same time and raise an emotional storm against it. He looked at the people about him in the bright city street, and from the expressions on young men's faces, even from the contour of shoulder and head of those walking in front of him, he could draw their conviction that he was right and should do this thing. Such a thought tainted his mind with a false resentment of evil, and he had an all but irresistible impulse to buttonhole someone passing in the street and fix him with this tale of a woman stricken to a narrow bed for ever and using her supreme intuition in realms she could never approach. And at the end, 'Do you not see her,' he could have cried, 'when the girl goes home and enters the room, how she looks? Those eyes, wild in a dread of disaster expected for years!'

They went to Cathcart and reached their favourite seat in the wood above the castle shortly after nine. No mention of his visit to Black Street was made until they were long settled and dusk was deepening into night. Jessie had the stealth of a young animal uncertain of its quarters. There was cunning in every word she uttered.

'I cannot sleep for thinking of Dundee, darling,' she murmured dreamily. 'You are taking me, aren't you?'

'No, dear, I've decided not. We couldn't.'

'Oh, but why, when we love?'

'I saw your mother tonight.'

'Umm. So you did go.'

'Yes.'

'But what on earth—what did she say?'

'It's not that. But, she's so helpless, somehow.'

'Darling, what has she got to do with it? Don't we love?'

'Yes, that's true.'

'You do love me?'

'Yes.'

'Well, it would be like getting married, wouldn't it?'

'It wouldn't be right.'

She held her breath, remembering early struggles. Then quietly she asked him, 'What did mother say?'

'She seemed sad. You didn't tell me how ill she was.'

'She's been ill so long.'

'So I heard.'

He recognized the moment's offer. Now was his chance to send her packing and have done with it. But her arm was round him and her cheek was close to his. Her beauty was made perceptible at a touch.

On the Friday night they met again. There was a picture they wanted to see up town, and after it, while the evening was yet young, they went into a café and ordered supper. She was happy and vivacious. She wore a new hat she had trimmed herself, and the whole thing, she computed, had cost only three shillings. It was of the shape she invariably selected, a wide brim arching her face and closing in quickly on her bobbed hair at the back. Over and over again he was called upon to say that it was beautiful.

Waiting for supper, she sidled up as near as she could at the table and whispered:

'I'm going to put it on tomorrow, darling, and my new blouse as well.'

Her eyes, smiling gleefully at first, became threatened with tears.

'You *are* taking me to Dundee, aren't you?'

He shook his head and looked past her to the wall beyond.

'Jessie, you shouldn't have left your mother!'

It came at last, unexpectedly, and in spite of his resolve to be silent. Perhaps it was the commercial tone and the overhanging dreariness of the café, filled with its aimless diners and coffee-drinkers, that quickened his temper. When it was said he remained gazing steadfastly past her.

'Why?'

No doubt she couldn't understand his sudden change and was startled by it. She must have decided that if he was going to cut up rough he would have done it last night in the wood. His tenderness there had placated her fears, even though he had said he was not going to Dundee. It didn't follow, to his mind, however, that she should change so swiftly and gather up her defences in one grip with that clipping word. Though he did not look, he knew her eyes had cleared of shadow and her whole frame become taut.

'Your mother seems to be a worrier. She was not a fit person to be left. You are young and strong. Your absence and your silence are agonies long drawn out. No irritation was sufficient cause for you to leave and forsake her.'

But was not this worlds and worlds worse than he had intended? Yet it came as something remembered which had to be said. He expected a following storm of weeping and an ultimate despair. But no. She must have perceived the source of genuine feeling from which he drew, and known instinctively that he would return and return to it. So she cut across his path with an affected misunderstanding.

'But we're going to send a letter, aren't we? I've got it written. Isn't that what we have arranged? Oh, this is dreadful!'

'Yes, it is. But you wouldn't have written had I left it to yourself.'

'How could I have written before?'

'In any case, I was talking of your having left the house at all. Had I known the real circumstances in Black Street I'd have been all against it.'

'What real circumstances? Didn't I tell you them? Didn't you see my father for yourself—my dear considerate father? What other circumstance but cruelty, drudgery from morn till night, and constant unceasing abuse!'

'That dear woman stricken for life to her bed. That should have weighed against all else. You left her to his mercy. If he is as bad as you say, it was your duty to protect your mother.'

'Protect her!' she breathed incredulously.

'You wouldn't have had my assistance had I known.'

And there was the mistake. As soon as he had uttered the word he knew he had blundered fatally. She narrowed her eyes and her lips shut tightly as she murmured, 'So!'

Angered by his own clumsiness and incapable of explaining it away, he turned on her fiercely, 'Don't sit swaying there like an idiot. You're not on a stage. There's nothing dramatic in your situation. It's just mean. What's the "So!" for?'

His voice was louder than he knew, and people at neighbouring tables turned round in astonishment. Their action attracted others farther off and a hush fell on the place. David cast a wild look about him. Of course, it had to be like this! What a hole to start a row in! All last night in the castle wood had been wasted kissing and petting her, and now that he was narrowed down to a small table in a café he called an audience of dissolute faces to gloat over a lovers' quarrel.

That word, assistance. It was the only word that could have made Jessie forget her whereabouts. The theatrics of her position were so vivid that the restraint of her dramatic sense failed her and she collapsed. Her head came forward suddenly and her arm bent under her face as she wept bitterly. Just then the waiter came along.

David's angry conviction was that she purposely took the worst meaning from the word. The money he had given her had been a mere trifle and was of no consequence. Anyone would have admitted that. She was his sweetheart, and she was, or thought she was, to be his wife. But the reference to it had been brutal and she was quick to make it diminish the moral advantage he held.

'Jessie,' he whispered, 'for God's sake, sit up. Here's the waiter.'

A sob, heartbreaking and incredibly loud, came from her hidden lips as she slithered from the table, lifting her head only slightly and sweeping round in a blind impetuous movement. Her sleeve was wet where her teeth had bitten into it. Her hat was pitched to one side. For a second she seemed to hesitate, became aware of the silence round her, and then, lurching from her chair to the door, she flew through the vestibule into Sauchiehall Street. David, hatless, mad with remorse and passion, dashed after her.

She escaped being run over by a motor-car only by the barest fraction of a second. The noise of rattling tram-wheels and the shriek from the motor's horn drowned David's agonized cry. By the time traffic allowed him to dart across the street she was gone.

Blindly she ran through the crowds on the pavement until she reached the first opening into darkness, one of those unlighted streets leading from the main thoroughfare into the desolate wastes of office buildings, darkened and shuttered for the night.

There were many streets such as this, long parallel lines going north to south and crossing over long parallel streets going east to west, making the place a patchwork of squares, each square honeycombed with inner lanes and tunnels. Being entirely unused for official purposes at night, this area was sparsely lighted and evil with inexplicable figures. Jessie's flight was more noticed in this empty zone than in the business of Sauchiehall Street.

In a lane between West George Street and West Regent Street he captured her. She gave up and sank exhausted against the wall. But she kept her face stubbornly away from him and she was sobbing still. In a moment the distant corners were alive with furtive shadows.

He was madly excited and he too was breathless, having on two occasions gone the wrong way, searching the lanes behind Bath Street and running fruitlessly along empty West Regent Street. Now he gripped her tightly and shook her, but her sobs broke dangerously and he quickly released her. He knew by her sobs that she had been weeping wildly as she ran. Alarm at her hysterical condition cleared his brain. He put an arm against the wall and stood in a sheltering attitude.

'Jessie, darling, be calm.'

At the four corners of the lane men had been gathering speculatively. Beyond the corners, on the street and far pavements, were still more. Someone, affecting an unconcerned gait and being impudent, came into the lane and strolled past with devilish meaning trailing after him. While he was near, Jessie's sobbing quietened and she stood motionless, a handkerchief pressed to her lips.

'Come, dearest, we must go,' David pleaded. '—These men.'

She pushed herself from the wall, gripped his hand when he attempted to touch her and threw it from her, and, huddling her shoulders in an involuntary shudder, looked after the retreating man.

'Come quickly, darling,' the gentle voice beside her insisted. 'Look at the ghouls!'

He took stock of such as he saw when ultimately they emerged from the lane. Jessie walked closely beside him with downcast head, the great brim of her hat completely shading her face. And as they went David kept up a constant murmur of supplication which was, however, but the dying shivers of his agitation and flowed with no effort. His eyes were on the men.

And he thought: any one of them would speak to Jessie if he left her now. They were all physically endowed as he was, but mentally irresponsible. Any one of them might turn up in the course of the day's business and he would speak to him, courteously, affably. Perhaps he had taken coffee from a cup one of them had used in a city restaurant. They might be what is called quite decent—like Clifford.

They walked downhill in Hope Street, skirted the Central Station and passed along Argyle Street under the railway bridge into Jamaica Street. On the bridge over the Clyde they stopped. David had taken her arm after being three times repulsed, and now she let it be. A crowd of people were watching the manoeuvres of a vessel, with funnel tilted back, on the black waters below. Jessie pulled his arm round and they leant against the broad marble parapet.

His eyes became fixed on the glittering array of lights heaped into the sky. Reflections were caught in the dark slimy water, giving a perforated design of bridges, buildings, docks and vessels, like bright beads sewn upon black velvet. The yellow points of gaslight in tenement and warehouse windows seemed isolated like lamps on unseen signals. Those yellow windows were elongated by the rippling river as though they were tiny steamers floating at anchor. They were crowded round with lesser lights of white and red and green from the railway, and all, save the red, once one's eyes had grown accustomed to them, revealed little zones of restless water. The red lights seemed to plunge and die anew in every passing wave.

Exhausted with weeping and running, Jessie stood like a child fascinated by these river lights. The taste of salt tears was in David's throat and he too was grateful for the pause. His spirit was slowly settling, and upon its smoothing surface the faint reflections of permanent things came creeping back.

'Isn't it beautiful, my darling?' he murmured.

She had not spoken once, and now she merely nodded. But it seemed she pressed his hand with her arm.

'Won't we push off and really have supper somewhere?' he ventured.

Reluctantly she eased away from the parapet, and David, in turning, caught sight of the person who had been standing close beside her. This man was leaning on the marble, his hands in his pockets and his face rather deliberately away from them. David recognized him immediately as one of the men who had been standing at the corner of the lane.

His mind was rocked back to its former agitation while he strove for position, getting his back ultimately to the man and delaying Jessie as innocently as he could.

'I wonder why they are so late with that boat,' he said, and on a sudden kicked violently backward, so that the heel of his shoe, iron-tipped, went deep into the man's leg.

There was a yell. The fellow's cap, old and flattened, like an unelevated opera-hat, at best but perilously poised on his close-cropped head, was tossed into the black gulf below. A crowd came surging round, thinking someone had jumped over.

David swung Jessie round and they made off swiftly. She didn't know what had happened. As they hurried away she looked back over her shoulder, wonderingly. She wanted to ask him if he knew, but she was sullen still.

As he walked down Eglinton Street with her a flock
of memories were winging round David. The kick at that
man had helped him immensely, and he was now prepared
to be tenderly sentimental. She had never been on these
pavements with him before. Yet they were sacred to her on
account of the times he had walked them going home after
lovely evenings with her in the Black Street days.

'I used to love this walk home after being with you,' he
whispered. 'Every part of the road is memorable for some
thought I've had about you, darling.'

She made no reply, for apparently she had been distracted by a showcase at the door of a shop. This thing had a
mirrored frame, and as Jessie swerved to catch a glimpse
of its contents a great standard light in the street lit up her
face brightly as daylight for David's eyes. When they were
beyond the mirror her head drooped as before.

Once more his reviving spirits were crushed. An unspeakable dreariness descended on him, for in that mirror he
had seen the dreaded twist of her lips, that sneer which was
as a blight that left nothing tender or warm within him. He
was suddenly inflamed with his old anger.

'I detest that smile! What do you mean by it?'

Shouting again. There was a tramcar passing and it was
murderously loud. He had to shout to be heard. But it was
heard as a shout. Reason perished in a flood of despising as
she gripped his hand and threw it from her once again. She
seemed to totter at his side.

The street lights were bleared by tears swimming in her
eyes. And all this was what they would afterwards call a
wasted night. He could see beyond to a time when she would
be quick and vivacious, giving him that slightly bewildering
feeling of having a child romping round him. That would
be when they were heading for some quiet place in wood or
gardens where he could gather her in his arms. There need
be no end to love-making with her. No end. But there was
another side to life and this was it, and the memory of this

might destroy the other. Would it? He sighed. Even now, perhaps, she might consent were he to lead her to a tram stop and take her to some sheltered corner in a suburban lane. There they might forget everything and afterwards go home, like tired children, to a deep sleep. In his weariness the picture was infinitely alluring, but he had not the strength to grasp at it.

Of all her conflicting emotions he knew the fear of being misunderstood was uppermost. Not even the enigmatic remark about the smile had such alarms, though it had further shocked her. He wanted to ask her where she thought she was misunderstood. Was he not, rather, finding her out? But she more than half believed he was not. She had manufactured her story of domestic misery, and so vividly had she imagined it, so believable had it appeared, that any disputing of it now summoned the actual emotion of being misunderstood and misbelieved.

They walked on in silence. He remembered a small restaurant somewhere near and kept a look-out for it. At last its yellow flare beckoned them, and as they slowed down at the door a gust of warm air enveloped them.

He nodded interrogatively, 'Will we?'

She glanced at his bare head and away again.

'You've no hat.'

With a shrug he answered, 'It doesn't matter. I'd be taking it off anyway. Come on.'

They passed meekly in and took a seat at a marble-topped table whose only ornaments were a shallow salt-cellar and a long-necked vinegar-bottle.

Each table was surrounded by high partitions of wood and coloured glass, and seats of plain cedarwood were affixed on both sides. A mirror flanked their table on the left, and the passage-way exposed them to a cubicle opposite where another mirror very possibly revealed them to unseen eyes in other parts of the shop. Looking at this far mirror they saw themselves repeated in unending rows into the depths of illusion. Big electric globes hung starkly from the midroof, the reflection of one, dazzlingly bright, appearing as an enormous star upon the tunic of Mussolini, whose portrait was suspended above a door marked 'Staff'.

From this door a young Italian girl approached them. The simple menu she had to forward had only one alternative to green peas and lemonade, and this they chose, fish and chips.

The service was good. In a few minutes the girl was back with plates heaped to the edges. She placed one before Jessie and the other she laid directly opposite on the other side of the table. Then she stood and smiled cheekily on them.

Her broad hint did much to restore order between them, and as David rose and sidled round the table to where he faced Jessie, the young Italian's lips flowed over her perfect teeth in an elaborate grin.

'If youse want anything else, give us a tinkle,' she said slowly, and moved away.

'You would say she spoke English perfectly, wouldn't you?' David smiled.

'It's dreadful,' Jessie replied. Her eyes lifted hesitantly to his.

Tears are such untidy things. Their refreshment is all inwardly. Her spirit was in her lovely eyes, abashed and veiled and timid as a nun's with an intercessionary shyness. Her lips were smooth and softly lined, her cheeks rounded in gentle curves. These were lovelinesses glimpsed through the disorder created by flowing tears. She looked like a city child home from an exhausting picnicking in the country. There was something of the dust of sadness about her. Her very fingers were grimy with much taking-off and pulling-on of gloves. A little handkerchief, crumpled and tear-soiled, which she now laid on the marble slab beyond her cup, was a pitiable little thing. Its delicacy was not meant for such distracted fingers.

David forgot the little Italian and her Glasgow lingo.
She had brought them face to face, and under the marble
top their knees were pressing tentatively. The indwelling of
their fondness for each other was recognized in tired eyes.

The warm tea first took a huskiness from her voice, and as
its influence spread her cheeks flushed ever so slightly. They
murmured their words and ate, to begin with, hesitantly,
but ultimately with a good relish. David rang the bell and
ordered more tea.

She spread her handkerchief on her lap, smoothing it out
with slow waves of her fingers. Then she crushed it into a
ball again, and, reaching over empty plates, whispered:

'Why did you do it?'

It was enough.

'I don't know.'

Her eyes clouded easily. 'And what did you mean about
my smile? What way did I smile? Why do you detest it?'

'Don't let us talk about it—just now.'

She sat back, pondering; then with an incredulous note,
she said:

'But you should have remembered what you had been
saying.'

'Yes, dear. I don't like the way you twist your lips
sometimes, that's all. It doesn't improve you.'

Her head was against the partition, the flowing brim of
her hat darkening her brows. The light of an electric globe
above but reached her lower lashes; the eyes were shaded.
She gave up the mystery of his words about her smile and
went back to earlier events which she was able to encompass
with a sigh. He did not mean them; he could not mean them;
there must be some mistake, for he was still loving and
compassionate. It was all so silly, so wrong of him.

When she leaned forward once more and the light flooded
her eyes, her gaze had an ardour that sent a thrill through
his blood. It was a mute supplication to wring the heart of
a man. It was more—more than that. It seemed to clutch at

him. It was as intangible as an inherited poise of the head, the flicker of an eyelash. But it was there, sure as mother-love, aye, sure as in the eyes of the mother tortured with doubts and fears.

That clutch came on him when his very core was salted with tears. In telling her what he hated in her he but exposed the eagerness of his love. She broke through into this and appealed to his love with her promise and allure of bodily beauty. Those eyes were young and fresh and haunting; the mother's dark and smouldering with the damped-down fires of impotent yearning. Goaded on by the mother's selfish questing, he had rebelled against the daughter's faithlessness and been met by the same pleading and the same questing in the young and lovely eyes.

What did she matter, that old worn-out body in her coffin-shaped room in Partick? What she wanted was a man for her daughter, so that she could lie there, and, when her time came, die in peace. Her innuendoes, her silences which had poured like black poison into his veins, her queer bullet-like questions and her suspicions were bundled up and thrown into a corner of the mind. He knew they were not permanently gone; but he needed the clearance. Jessie's eyes were shining into his; her lips were parted in a rapt expression as though she were listening to far-off music. They lingered on, and slowly their hands crept below the marble to grasp upon the hidden community of knees. So were they lost in each other until a smothered giggle somewhere sent them shattering through the silence into the hubbub of their self-conscious selves.

She said their love had triumphed that night and that as a result of the row they had been brought closer than ever together. The taste of tears was still in her throat when she said it, but her eyes were bright. She was loath to let him go, begging a few more minutes and then some more during which they went over once more the outlines of their talk and promises. She had agreed to write a letter

to her parents which he would take the following morning
to Dundee. No further mention of their week-ending was
made. Instinctively she knew that their making-up—which
was like tender skin upon a bruise—would not stand the
strain. He was going to Dundee alone, and as he would be
able to catch an early train—Saturday was a short day in the
office—he would be back in Glasgow and over at her room in
Langside before teatime. He was to meet her in the morning
and get the letter.

When at length she reached her room she sought out pen
and paper and scribbled down a few lines. He had told her
not to make it elaborate or effusive; she was to imagine she
actually was in Dundee and write as she might have done
under the circumstances. And she knew exactly what to do.

> Dear F. & M. [she wrote],
> I hope Mother is not having any bad turns and
> that you are doing all right. I am all right. This is
> a nice place but lonely sometimes. It is much quieter
> than Glasgow. I think I could take down that velvet
> dress, the black one, in your wardrobe, Mother. I will
> be to see you some day on my afternoon off and get it
> then. They are wearing dresses longer now. My blue
> petticoat won't do any longer because I had to add a
> bit already. Such a job it was. Hope Kate is sending
> things to the laundry if she can't wash for you. How is
> she? Can't tell when I will be but will be soon.
> > Much love,   J.

She read it over, put it in an envelope which she left
unsealed, and then prepared for bed.

By the writing of that letter—and the promise to write
others later, for David had got in touch with a man in
Dundee who would perhaps act as receiver and sender of
letters at his address—she had shown a willingness to do
what she could for her parents. She would never refuse to

do anything that might help them. She was not vindictive. She did not keep up a grudge. Would David realize that and stop worrying her? Had his refusal of her suggestion of week-ending something to do with her parents, or, more subtly, her attitude to them? For a moment there was a cessation of feeling as she considered this, which made David seem in his masterful way to be withholding his favours. She froze at the thought. But surely that could not be! She remembered earlier days when his tempestuous ardour all but swept every guard away, and then she smiled. No. He was in love now, really and truly in love, and wanted to obey love's rules.

Yet when she had put the light out and was lying in utter darkness in that quiet room, she conceded herself a certain disappointment. It was not that they were not going to Dundee: it was David himself. To behave like that was rather silly. If she told any of the girls in the shop about it they would say without hesitation that he didn't care for her. Whereas he really cared too much. He respected her. But it was rather silly of him to become so calculating, so careful. It was partly his abandoned way of treating her at the beginning that had fascinated her, for she believed, as though it were the only superstition left to woman, that a man had one inability, one supreme need, which was a failing, and that he had to be petted and comforted when refused. Let a man show himself superior to this failing and something of the appeal of his sex faded in the woman's mind.

The door at Black Street opened but a few inches in response to his knock on the following Monday evening, and, instead of the burly figure of Mr Adair, a small girl wedged herself within the narrow slit, her face peering mistrustfully at him. 'Mr Adair's no' in,' she whispered.

He got his foot against the door.

'I've come to see Mrs Adair; tell her I am here, please.'

The girl pressed the door and he withdrew his foot. It closed and the sneck fell shut. 'Wait an' Ah'll see,' she was murmuring as the face disappeared.

In a moment she was back and this time the door was opened, albeit grudgingly, to let him squeeze in. It fell shut behind him.

'Just go in.' David looked at the girl and wondered if she were capable of anything above a whisper. She returned his gaze almost friendlily, her eyes those of a little gossip seeking an understanding. He nodded and she smiled slyly.

'Well,' he greeted Jessie's mother brightly as he entered the room, 'you've got a capable doorkeeper. No fear of intruders here. How are you keeping today?'

She was propped up by a bed-rest, a coarse thing of wire netting encased in boards. A yellow shawl was thrown over the back of this and a bolster was wedged longways across it to support her head. Her hands were free.

'I'm just the same, no worse and no better.' The voice had its usual snap. 'There's no bettering for me.'

'One could get used to that thought if there was no danger of getting worse,' he murmured uncomfortably. His eyes searched for the letter which he had somehow imagined would be lying near this bed.

She did not keep him waiting long.

'See under my pillow there—that stupid girl put the letter there. As if I could get at it in such a place! I want you to look at it.'

The pillow's end, bulging with the weight of one side of the bed-rest, yawned above the mattress, its strings loosened and showing a blue-striped tick within. David pushed his hand underneath and grasped the letter.

There it was, the historic envelope, with its unfamiliar address in Jessie's familiar handwriting. He had thought of that in the train on Saturday. This was the first time he had seen her writing dedicated to someone else. He tried to look at it easefully.

'What's that postmark on the envelope?' the voice snapped out.

David looked at the postmark carefully and ground his teeth. Dearly then would he have loved to crush the face of some Dundee post-office servant under his heel, for the work of obliteration had been done with extreme slovenliness. The stamp was smudged at the top right-hand corner, showing only the beginnings of the official cancellation. Such a stamp could be taken off the envelope, washed, snipped, and used again.

For something to say he suggested this in a bantering fashion. Arguments to put to her gathered in his mind. How was the sender of this letter to know it would not be properly marked? How could the sender possibly arrange to have it smeared in this way? 'I often see envelopes like this,' he smiled. And then, 'What does she say?'

'But the postmark? That might have come from any-where.'

'But isn't Jessie in Dundee? Haven't I told you she is, and doesn't she say so herself?'

She was sullenly silent for a moment.

'Funny thing it should just have happened with that letter.'

'The postmark? I'd never have noticed.'

'I thought you said you often see it? But it doesn't matter. Mr Adair's not seen it yet. I'll see what he says. He won't be in till late tonight. That's Kate I've got. She comes for an afternoon and evening once a week.'

He looked about him to see if Kate had done anything to the room, but it was as usual. At the back of his mind for the past few days he had carried the idea of offering old Adair some help with the housework, and conceiving it now as a good breakaway from an irritating and disappointing subject, he assumed his best bedside manner.

'Would you be offended, Mrs Adair, if I offered to help Kate with the work? Seeing that Mr Adair is to be late? I could tidy your room, perhaps, and do some dusting.'

The dark eyes widened and the reflection of the entire window-frame behind him was caught in them, blinding out expression. They were dark luminous points of light.

But her voice betrayed her awakened emotion.

'Tuts, boy,' it murmured, 'what would you be doing that for!'

Eagerly he followed it up. 'I'd love to help you. Even for Jessie's sake and because she cannot do it herself. But apart from her, for your sake.'

'I never heard the like!'

'Oh, that's nothing. I often do it at home.'

She was completely bowled over. With a little shiver of delight he peeled off his coat and went into the lobby. Then he looked in again, smiling gaily. 'What fun! Where will I get a duster? From Kate?'

'Yes—oh yes,' she started. Her face was flushed.

In the kitchen Kate was drying a trayful of dishes.

'Can you give me a duster?' he asked her briskly.

With her gasp 'A whit?' she let the towel dangle from her fingers. She stood fixed, looking at him.

'I want a duster, please,' he expanded pleasantly. There were two drawers below the dresser, usual places for odds and ends in a kitchen, and he approached these. 'Perhaps I'll get one here.'

'Yes,' she whispered.

The drawer he drew open had cloths in all stages of dirtiness. He selected the least soiled and pushed back the drawer. Then, smiling upon the captivated Kate, he made to leave the place.

But she found her power of movement and sprang toward him.

'Whit's it for?' she breathed.

'I'm going to tidy up Mrs Adair's room. Don't worry, I'm not doing you out of your job.'

'I like that,' she sneered. 'If ye need the bucket and the scrubber's well, just let us know.'

'I shall.'

She had rounded him so that the light of the window was in her eyes. But she was not far enough away to have the whole design described to a pin-point. Rather it was that the light gave intelligence to the temper animating the eyes, insipid blue, with pale feeble-looking lids.

'I made the suggestion myself, you know,' he whispered, and quickly found a shilling in his pocket to slip to her. She took it as though she were disappointed with herself.

Armed with the duster, he passed through to Mrs Adair's room.

'You know,' she began at once, 'the dirt that comes seeping through those windows—you wouldn't believe it!'

'I'm sure so.'

'And there's no keeping of the curtains clean.'

It was of the curtains she seemed particularly ashamed. But the whole room was wretchedly unclean. There was a surface smoothness, one might say, as though a negligent hand brushed over things occasionally to deceive the casual eye. Underneath, and in corners, behind chairs and curtains, and along the edges of the window, was grime and filth.

In a moment he was back in the kitchen demanding the bucket and the scrubber. They heated a pail of water and Kate discovered some coarse soap in the press and an old rag that might make a respectable clout. There was one she had been using herself at the sink, but presumably it was too disreputable.

And so a long night of hard work began. Mrs Adair protested fiercely when he appeared, covered by an old overall, a blue print thing Jessie possibly was wearing that far-off night when he watched her slip downstairs with the ashes. But he was hilarious and optimistic of his abilities to wash a floor. Not only the floor was scrubbed, but the paintwork as well, and all the panellings below the window. Kate slipped to the door several times to watch open-mouthed. When the day was gone the work continued by gaslight. Chairs and wardrobe and bedstead were polished, pictures taken down and dusted, the mantelpiece washed and dried, and, last of all, the fireplace scrubbed.

They removed the bed-rest and Mrs Adair was pushed down flat among the blankets. When she was thoroughly covered and guarded against draughts, David got busy with the window. As a compromise with the expostulating woman, he allowed Kate to hold his knees while he sat on the windowsill and cleaned the outside. Black Street, with its lemon-coloured lights in a narrow row, its lighted windows one and two storeys high, seemed to sway perilously in and out of a black gulf as he glanced downwards. His feet pressing strongly against the woodwork within, he thrilled at the remoteness of his perch.

When all was done the bed was seen to have suffered shame. The freshness and new glitter around exposed its shabbiness.

'Haven't we a clean bedspread, now?' he asked kindly. 'Just to make things complete?'

Mrs Adair looked imploringly at Kate.

'I'll see what's to do in the kitchen, and Kate can do the bed,' he laughed.

They discussed the thing quickly when he was gone, and Kate, moving with unusual alacrity, produced clean pillow-slips and a new cover that had a pleasant blue edge, and a white valence. These refreshed his eyes when he returned, on Kate's invitation. Grinning sheepishly, she stood behind him with the discarded linen in her arms.

'Well,' he said smiling, 'you look better now.'

'You're a warrior!' The voice had a softness new to him, and her eyes, so ready to challenge his at all times, now kept looking about her furtively as though the room's cleanliness were a nakedness that shamed her.

'We'll not be long now,' he cried in high spirits, and whisked Kate out of the room with her bundle of clothes. They lit a feeble gas-jet in the bathroom and washed those soiled bed-things and then hung them on the kitchen pulley. They made up Mr Adair's bed, which was in a recess in the kitchen, and dusted down the walls and mantelpiece. Occasionally as they worked their hands touched; they nudged each other, held the rickety steps securely for one another, passed an occasional glance and grin. She had come to regard it all as a joke, and, on remarking that she was kept late, got another shilling out of the job. Her whispering voice improved as their acquaintance ripened. She was ultimately disposed to giggle.

And his reward, when he came to take his leave of the woman in her clean bedroom, was a smile from those terrible dark eyes. The smile sweetened and enriched the face, making it younglike, making it confusingly womanly. It did not only express gratitude: it revealed a corner of her mind where she still remembered days when smiles and kindly glances were of the habit of life. He saw far back behind those eyes in that moment, and knew that he had become linked up in her mind with a happiness of the long ago.

PART FIVE

The Final Test

The thought that he had brought some comfort to this woman relieved him in moments when the comic spirit was upon him and he saw things as they really were, a fit subject for the laughter of such pleasant people as Elizabeth and Clifford. Apart from his concern for the woman, the situation during the next few weeks became ludicrous. What could be more absurd than the picture of Jessie, apprenticed to the profession of being a lady and lodged in a comfortable Langside home, being ignorant of the fact her sweetheart was snatching hours from her company to visit the house she had abandoned and assist a slut of a girl in the housework? It was of the very spirit of comedy.

There might have been some satisfaction gained had Jessie been told. She would not have been expected to enjoy the comedy, but she might have perceived her position and been touched to shame. Jessie, however, knew no more of his gallantry than Elizabeth or Clifford, and he withheld news of it from her for precisely the same reason as kept him silent elsewhere. As they would have laughed him to scorn, so she would have scorned him with her sneer. Already she had brought against his veiled accusations of selfishness a trace of contempt. Her ability to reduce him by insinuations of coarseness and childishness was growing. She could not ultimately hide a worldly contempt for the timid and unsophisticated.

Perhaps it was not contempt so much as a lowering of tolerance, such as she came to reveal for the memory of his attitude regarding the week-end. His refusal then had been a bewildering twist away from the natural order of things, and knowing this he had been strenuous in his protestations of affection. He knew she accepted these protestations, but in spite of them she never recovered her old abandon in love-making. The possession she had to offer, which all girls of her kind think inescapable in its power, had been reduced to the level of her other appeals.

As the days passed there thus came to be ranged round him as fixed points of his consciousness, Elizabeth, Clifford, Jessie, Mrs Adair, each locked in a selfishness nothing could break up. They were set in their maturity and had no compromise to offer him. How amusing, could Clifford but know of it, that he who had suddenly found himself liberated from moral scruples learned in boyhood, was now slightly suspect by a young girl for not accepting his liberty! He had not and he never would escape these boyish scruples. He had inherited from them a tenderness upon which anyone could play, a tenderness in which he believed with an amazing optimism in ultimate recognition. Every one of them, Elizabeth, Jessie, Clifford, and the woman in Black Street, bruised that tenderness repeatedly; but they did not know it was there. There must be something in each of them that his indifference could equally offend.

Both the daughter and mother had the same commanding power over him. When he was with Jessie he understood her reasons as obvious human failings. She had realized that she cared for him and had fastened upon him desperately to achieve a life of love and comparative ease. As her home could never become the background for such a life she had forsaken it. It was simple enough. So, too, was the situation at Black Street, where the woman clutched at him as at a turn of fortune, a lucky chance. But she was more complicated than her daughter, for as he opened out before her as desirable, she was conscience-stricken. The native decency of the woman struggled to tell him to go away for his own sake. From her first fear that he was a rogue out to imperil her daughter, she had come to a fear that her daughter might bring him woe.

Discovering this in her, he should have taken it as a final sign of danger and gone away. As it was, it remained at the back of his mind during his long indecision like a last refuge. It lay behind the excitement of Jessie's allure and was temporarily obliterated every time they idled together on a country road or lay lazily in an Eaglesham field. Then her beauty and compassion worked upon his imagination like the blossoming of summer which they saw opening all about them. Her sweetness was physical as the beauty of flowers and sunset colours on the moors, but as these it was the expression of something else that would survive her youth. He could not dissociate the flesh and the spirit as the world of Clifford did, and saw in the beauty of the girl's body a promise whose fulfilment must be of the spirit.

Yet there had been those blinding doubts which led him to Partick, where he discovered a state of affairs entirely different from what she had described. That was of her spirit, of her heart. His only excuse for her was that she feared he would be repelled by such a house, or at the least that their love would suffer from the unimaginative attitude of her parents. Suppose, then, he showed her that he could withstand that house, that he was without snobbery, that he was willing, in his love of her, to share her responsibility for these people; what then?

Such a proposition, it seemed to him, closed in upon her like a trap. There was no escape for her if he were dexterous enough in his methods. It would be a trap in which her character would be finally tested, and round it would be the magnanimity of his own heart. So he thought it out very thoroughly, making it an excuse for suspended action while enjoying their tender love-making which was almost a routine in their daily lives.

Jessie went into the trap when at length he was ready, prepared by experience to countenance anything from this strange lover. They had taken a 'bus to Waterfoot one evening and wandered along 'Hedges', a favourite road wending over the hill to Thorntonhall. It was a calm end to a moody day, with a diamond sky that had no flash of sun nor horizon of colour; all was one stretch of white in varying intensities of space and cloud. The green woods and hedges and green-brown fields were dustless and cool-scented after rain at afternoon. Small white gates at the corners of fields were still beaded with raindrops, and here and there on the brown road a cluster of raindrops lay as though embedded in the earth where a recent breeze had shaken a lazy bough overhead. Feasting her eyes on all this, Jessie found her dreams clarified. This was what she wanted, this peace, with a cool room at the end of the road where a table, close to a window, was lit by candles or a lamp, with a white shade exquisitely embroidered. There she would sit, with David opposite. . . .

She turned to him with kittenish playfulness. She shook his arm because he was inclined to be silent, and ever so delicately she teased him with fears of his coldness and propriety.

'How's the agent in Dundee?' she whispered.

He stopped her then and kissed her lips madly. But she emerged still smiling at the question and with the teasing light still in her eyes. He shook her, lifted her in his arms and buried his face in her blouse.

'Darling, don't torture me,' he pleaded. 'Not that way; I love you too much.'

She sobered as she looked into his eyes.

'But you mustn't be afraid, dearest; there should be no restraint between us.'

'You wait!' he vowed.

She slipped to her feet again. 'Darling! Soon?'

'Yes. But how soon depends on you as much as on me.

Let's talk about it.'

They started walking again slowly. 'For me?' she asked. 'Why, I'm ready now.' Her voice changed in the next breath to entreaty. 'Oh, if only you'd take me away somewhere—away from Glasgow altogether, where we could start life afresh.'

'Afresh? Why, what is wrong that we need to start afresh?'

'I mean—life with you should mean a clean start all over again.'

He laughed at her.

'Why, I love Glasgow and wouldn't dream of leaving it. And besides, my job is here.'

'You are so clever, David, you'd get a job anywhere. London, for instance. Then we could live in the country and you could travel into town every day.'

'The idea's mad. We've got other people to think about. Your parents. . . . '

'Oh, them!' she pouted. 'Why do you keep on talking about them? You'd think they were your folk.'

'But they are yours, Jessie, and that's as good. And, of course, there's Elizabeth and the others.'

'They've got their own interests. If they wanted to go away they would leave us jolly soon.'

'They'd have their reasons, then. We have none. For the life of me I cannot think of one.'

'If you'd had the life I have had you'd hate the place. I see reasons all right.'

'You do talk nonsense, darling. Haven't you escaped all that—drudgery? You're happy now, aren't you? You will get to love Glasgow yet.

'And besides,' he went on, 'haven't we promised all these places we love so well—this road, and Eaglesham and Loch Lomond, to visit them after we're married and get our revenge?'

'We could come to them on holidays,' she pleaded.

'Think of it: in a new town, all alone, everything as fresh and new as our married life; free to be alone with no danger of interruption and no criticism, no anything.'

She was in a glow of excitement as she spoke, her eyes earnest in their promise of the joy she would give him. The whole energy of her young body was strained to give effect to her words. To her the idea of a new beginning was wholesome in its prospect of having her sins washed white as snow. Marrying and settling down in Glasgow, she would have no chance of escape from scenes of past mistakes.

But he was patient in his refusal, and although his words, remembered afterwards, seemed brief and clipping, they were spoken tenderly.

'We can't leave Glasgow, Jessie. There are things to be done. You must trust me in this.'

Then followed the test he had planned. It was better to bring it on now when her mind was in this state. The way he propounded it made it seem like an ultimatum. As he spoke she withdrew herself gently from his arms, as though, being separate, she could the better consider what he said.

'As far as I see it, darling, there's two ways open to us. We can wait two more years and gather enough to get a nice house somewhere round about here, or we can marry in a few months' time and take a house not so expensive. (Think of it, Jessie, in a few months!) In both cases we could take your mother and father with us. I wouldn't care about going to live with them in Black Street. And there is no room for us there. But there's plenty of fine houses to be had nowadays where your mother could have an airy open bedroom with a window looking out on green fields, perhaps. . . .

'I know you're going to say, "But didn't I leave them?" And it's natural enough. But you left because of reasons that would disappear once we are married. Is that not so? It would make you so happy to have your mother with you where you could look after her and at the same time be mistress of your own home! Of course, if Elizabeth married, she'd go away from Cornfoot Avenue and we could have it. Think of your mother in the bedroom over the back garden, looking across the city!'

There was nothing on earth Jessie would less willingly think about. She was frozen cold inside, the prospect of her whole life changed by his words, so that when she looked round furtively she found the green-and-white world grey and drab in its lack of sun. David, who had coaxed himself into believing in the idea, if only for the moment, went on talking.

'That poor paralysed body, it hasn't been warmed by the sun for fourteen years. Think of her in a light and airy room! We'd have a wireless installed at her bedside and a series of mirrors fixed, so that looking from her pillow she could see into the garden and also into the hall beyond her door. We'd maybe get a chair into which she could be lifted, eh?'

'Oh, I couldn't! I couldn't!'

She broke through the icy grip that held her and cried pitiably, 'I couldn't! No girl could. No girl wants a houseful of people when she's just married. And then Father—oh, are you mad! You don't understand.'

'I understand, Jessie,' he said harshly; but at the same time he caressed her arm lovingly. 'You had a rotten time in that house. But think—what conditions! Your father, poor, and you, my darling, rather extravagant, of course. Your mother paralysed and lying helpless in a nasty coffin-like room. What else could happen but bad tempers and misunderstanding and hate?'

She shook herself free once more. But he went on: 'It would all be different at Cornfoot Avenue. Your father wouldn't need to come home to work at dishes and floors and so on. He could gad about and enjoy himself; do something in the garden, maybe. And your mother'd be well looked after and content. She's a worrier, you know. But she'd learn not to worry once we were all together.'

He could not foresee what would happen now, but he was convinced that something would turn up to liberate her from this ghastly proposition. Then he would be free. Then he would summon the memory of his own mother and make an honest account of what he had done. But if, by some superhuman effort, she accepted this thing; if after a struggle she emerged triumphant over her selfish promptings and said, 'Yes, I'll do it,' he would elevate her at once to the level of mother-memory, mix her up with the elements of his life and cease from troubling her any more. For then she would have vindicated herself, and natural piety would make yet more beautiful her girlish love. It would be a matter of little difficulty for him then to arrange for her father and mother to be cared for by a housekeeper in some decent locality, while Jessie would have her own home to herself.

Could she have divined this as his scheme what marvellous acting that thick-hedged road would have seen! But he was strange; he had the most fantastic notions; and he had an infinite capacity for self-denial. She believed that he meant every word he uttered and that he was blandly certain she would ultimately agree.

With drawn lips, her voice trembling slightly, she gave him her answer.

'I could never do that, David.'

How subtly she got her warning into her voice! It was spoken on the level of the discussion, yet it stabbed underneath and made further talk hopeless. Her 'David' was like a recall of her independence.

But she was shaken. Fear and temper were racking her. She looked down on the sweeping meadowland cut into deeply by the main Eaglesham road, where like impossible snails long dark 'buses crawled; she strained her eyes to distinguish the clock on Clarkston Church and found relief in the rich level green of the tree-tops surrounding it; these composed the background to daydreaming in a cave-like shop. Was she to lose it all yet once again?

Never before had her hate of father and mother burned so fiercely. It was parching her, making her long for some succulent essence of real life, some thought or prospect of hope that would freshen her like wine.

They walked on in silence. He too was viewing the sweep of meadowland, his eyes running along the clear outlines, marking one familiar spot after another, and taking stock of all he saw as though conscious of manufacturing memories. He knew that he was torturing her. He was forcing this thing upon her, coldly, brutally; no pain of the flesh could equal what her mind was enduring. Yet this thought made no difference to his response when he looked over the fields to the quiet woods or upon the quiet sky.

They reached a spot where the road dips down into a shallow valley and breaks through a double file of trees. Here it was their custom to forsake the road and climb over the empty fields to a grassy hollow remote even from the light of the sky. Instinctively their pace slackened, but neither spoke until they were well past their place, and then she turned to him, broken.

'Don't let us quarrel again; I can't stand it.'

'Darling, why should we quarrel?' he replied easily. 'We're bound to disagree at first on some things. Come,' he grasped her hand lightly and they wheeled round: 'let's go over the fields.'

Twilight came and shut them in the grassy hollow, and they made their way home at last under the light of the stars.

It was always this way. He would look ahead to a situation developing and see there his opportunity of withdrawing. But when the time came he adjusted himself to the changed conditions and clung on, irresolute, still fascinated by her physical charm and the little intangible associations of the spirit.

The situation here, however, had been subtly advanced beyond his expectation, for in his acting of the part with her he had felt his proposal so vividly that her emphatic denial promoted the actual feelings of frustration. There was anger and hate at the centre of a disappointment he had once thought might be insipid with generosity.

In this anger he was interested; and once again he had the notion of himself as someone standing apart and watching. He could visualize the whole thing as upon a mental stage whereon he was scheming and she in her defence thwarting him; he could see her betray herself before his cunning and yet remain unshrinking because she was his equal or superior in her eagerness for love. His sympathy was touched to tenderness when he saw how blindly she strove to keep him wholly and entirely to herself. And then his anger would blaze at her for her wanton selfishness, and the whole cycle of his thought revolve again.

The question of holidays was facing them as the summer days came on. There was a spell of fine weather, and June came from the lily light of mild May weeks with a slowly intensifying heat. Cornfoot Avenue sweltered in the sun and smelt of greenery, and tar was blistered on the roadways. The sky above Glasgow seemed of an endless altitude, a great dome fixed and unalterable. The glimpses of beauty above and around them made town folk eager to be away.

Jessie's holidays were due at the middle of July, coinciding with the period Elizabeth had chosen, and David was faced with the prospect of disappointing one of them. Both knew that he would get away from the office whenever he wished, so that, while Elizabeth was assuming he would accompany her as usual and that they had only the problem of place to decide upon, Jessie was impatient that they should go somewhere together, to a boarding-house at the coast where ever so many young couples spent their holidays nowadays. He knew that when it came to the last minute he would tell Elizabeth he was going with Jessie unless, before that time, he could bring this invisible dispute between them to a head. Through his magnanimity there was a streak of cowardice, and against his tenderness, in which, if anything, he prided himself, there was a harshness like alternating waves in shot silk. He could not contemplate forsaking Jessie for a fortnight while they were still friends, but he could hasten the climax to their hidden feud so that he might by holiday-time be rid of her altogether!

He was preparing for an emergency of strength within him by which he could cast her off, and the immediate thing to be done, it seemed to him, was to redeem Jessie in the eyes of her parents. By doing this he would be expiating a wrong for which he was partly responsible. His task, then, was to make Black Street a welcoming place against Jessie's returning, so that she could take up her domestic ties where she dropped them. Better than that: she would find her relations improved and strengthened by his good offices. Then would the loss of him be minimized, and then it would not matter what her mother thought of him. She would have her daughter restored to her without injury and all would be well.

Each time he went to Black Street he found the invalid's brow still stern, but cleared of its storm. Other letters had come from Dundee with perfectly obliterated stamps and with an address which Mr Adair had verified in one of the reference-rooms in the public library. The woman had a ready smile for her visitor, and her questions were softened by a new respect.

It was to the man, however, that David turned with some apprehension. What did he think of the Dundee address and what was his reaction to this visiting? Mr Adair's simplicity was as apparent as his wife's integrity. His docility and girth gave him a grotesque appearance which might at first repel a stranger. There was nothing evil in the man. Even to himself his simplicity was mostly stupidity. 'You never know' was one of his sickly phrases, but he was too fat and too lazy ever to set about getting to know. He would say, 'Ach, this stomach's like a barrel!' being in this no worse than many a more energetic man; and he would pat it gently as though it were something to be humoured. He thought of Jessie with the same lassitude, considering only the extra work she had left him. Beyond that and an instinctive dislike of her display of fineness, his mind was untouched by her. Not in a hundred years would he have gone of his own volition to verify the Dundee address.

This David confirmed one evening after a few minutes' talk with him in the kitchen, and as his confidence strengthened his interest waned, for if the man was unsuspicious he was negligible.

The woman in the bed, however, insisted that her husband was equally alive to the situation which was developing. 'Mr Adair is so grateful to you for helping us,' she whispered on this same occasion. '—And the flowers, too.' Later on she reverted to the same subject. ' "My!" he said, "it must be fine to keep a clean house." But, you know, a man can't both look after a house and do his day's work outside. Kate helps a bit, but she's slow. And he says she dirties one place while cleaning another.'

'She seemed a bit like that,' David murmured. 'It's a pity you couldn't have a housekeeper here all the time.'

The eyes gleamed their old light of self-interest and her voice was argumentatively loud as she elaborated on this.

'Now, how could we have that? Where's the money to come from? The man's done. He can't go about as much as he used to do, and he's only paid for what he gets. He's no' on a salary like most folk hereabouts. He's no good at climbing stairs, or walking, for that matter, and the poor soul's losing his old customers. Is it right that his pay should drop when he's tired or ill, or when an old customer goes away or dies? The manager's all right: he draws his salary and never goes out at all. Housekeeper? The man's got enough to do to pay the rent and taxes.'

'I'm sorry. I didn't know he was a commission man. Jessie didn't tell me. She never mentioned his business.'

The woman nodded, her lips shutting close. She was still full of her subject.

'Oh no, we canna afford anything like that.'

Perhaps she was thinking that it was just as well to tell him these facts at once and so clear away any false ideas that Jessie's talk had suggested. There was a glint of loyalty to her husband in this, and the look she gave the man when a few minutes later he slithered in was eloquent of her feelings for him.

'Now, now,' she protested, 'you're no' doing too much, are you?'

David was on his feet.

'Please let me help. I'd love to, really.'

'Tuts, tuts, there can't be much to do. Sit down and don't fash yourself.'

'Ay,' Mr Adair murmured a little ruefully, 'I'll no' be long. Were you wanting a cup of tea?' he asked her.

'Yes; let's all have one in here,' exclaimed David. 'I'll come and help.'

'Oh, come awa', then, if ye must; but she'd as soon ye sat and gassed.'

David smiled and winked to her as he passed out. There was this secret between them now, that the poor man was tired. It justified his leaving her.

In the kitchen they gathered the cups and saucers upon a tray and buttered some fingers of bread while waiting on the kettle to boil. Standing at the gas-ring Mr Adair whispered:

'She'll be speiring you about Jessie, eh?'

'No,' David replied briskly. And then, 'At least, not much.'

'Ay. She'll be wanting to know if ye're going to marry her, I suppose.'

In his slow animal fashion he cared for that ·stricken woman. The way he framed his questions showed his own indifference, and the value of the answers lay entirely in their power to influence her. David found it difficult to believe in himself before that indifference. It amounted to an unconscious despising. Yet because of the man's concern for the woman it was impossible to trifle with the questions.

'Are ye?' he was asked.

It was almost man to man. Or taking advantage of the man-to-man attitude.

'Yes, I am; I mean to talk to you about that.'

'Oh ay.'

The kettle was singing. Mr Adair poured some water into the teapot to heat it, and having rinsed this out reached for the caddy. He was a father and was to be approached regarding his daughter's marriage. Knowing his daughter and her respect for him, he crept into his shyness at once. 'Oh ay,' he repeated. 'That's what the missis was wondering. Ye'll be telling her.'

He gave his wife her tea in an invalid's cup, fastening her fingers upon the crook. She placed the stem on her lips and sucked slowly. When she was not drinking her tongue licked the smooth edge reflectively.

David seated himself at the window. The man's questions, echoes from the woman's talk, crystallized the position neatly enough. No fellow who did not intend to become a son of the family would have visited as he had or behaved in such a manner during the visits. He was expected to speak, and the longer he put off the more absurd any speech would be. As it was, he had time enough to put everything right: he had a month yet before holiday-time. . . .

'I was telling Mr Adair that Jessie has promised to marry me. I thought I'd better find out if you approve.'

The little nervous laugh which followed this revealed that he knew how willingly they would approve. It was the first note of superiority he had sounded in that room, and of it, more than of the intelligence he was conveying, he was immediately ashamed.

The woman made no movement, save with her eyes, which had turned in the direction of her husband. From where David sat the whites were prominent, but the expression of serious joy she had for the man thrilled him. There shone the triumph of days and weeks of patient prayer.

'Of course,' he went on, 'we've nothing fixed. It's not easy with Jessie being in Dundee. So we're thinking that she should come home again and then she'd get on quicker with her arrangements.'

They were both looking at him diffidently. Mrs Adair was alert to his every word, weighing it against her knowledge of Jessie to get an exactitude of meaning, and at the same time cherishing a hope that things might be better than she knew. Even the man seemed to sense the importance of the hour and kept his gaze unaccustomedly direct.

'But,' David interrupted himself with a laugh, 'I'm maybe premature. I should ask for your permission, shouldn't I?'

The woman's eyes smiled on him. 'Don't mind us,' she said quietly. With difficulty she tilted toward her husband. 'You are glad to hear of this, aren't you, William?'

'Oh ay, they should do no' so bad.'

There was a moment's awkward pause. They had obviously nothing to say. They did not trust themselves sufficiently to enlarge on the news. And for the nonce David was unable to steer the thing safely on what would have been conventional lines. Instead, there came to him in a flash the thought that this was the opportunity he had been seeking. He was but nosing out the full possibilities of his chance even as he accepted it, his eyes smiling mildly upon the set face in the bed.

'There is just one thing she is talking about that you ought to know,' he began slowly and evenly; 'she's worried about you. We don't feel that we can let you stay here indefinitely without assistance. Jessie's suggestion is that we all stay together somewhere. We might pool our resources, as it were. She could have a maid to help her, and then she'd have plenty of time for her playacting and so on. If we got a decent house, Mrs Adair, you'd have a big room to yourself with an interesting window, perhaps. Trees in the garden, you know, wireless, and so on. It would be cheerier for you, wouldn't it?'

Lucid and gentle as his voice had been, the embarrassment his words created was a severe physical strain upon his elders. Two spots of red burned on the woman's cheeks and her eyes looked hot and glazed. Mr Adair had laid down his cup and now sat with his arms on his knees gazing at the floor.

Looking on them in this acute tension, when even the sluggish emotions of the man were being freshly stirred, David was fired with a wild sympathetic yearning 'that it was only so!' He was a ghoulish fiend to sit there playing with poor people's feelings, secure, as he knew, in the thought that soon he might be free of them for ever. What a half-blind cad he was! This view of suffering people having their eyes turned toward the light was a new experience to him! How much more glorious life would have been had he really meant to carry out the picture he was idly, wantonly painting for them. At the moment, in their inarticulate excitement, they seemed the most lovable people on earth.

'Have you been thinking that?'

The voice of the woman was shrill from a dry throat.

'Yes.'

'Not that we would come, you know, but . . . '

Mr Adair had risen, forewarned of the effect of her

emotions, and was but in time to grasp the drinking-cup from her fingers that on a sudden had twisted as with a palsy. When he withdrew and David looked upon her again her lips were drawn downward, stricken by a soundless wail.

'There now,' Mr Adair muttered, his back to her and stooping to pick up his cup, 'there, there, there!'

But it burst upon them ultimately, a pitiful howl, breaking the transfixed look of her face, and bringing with it a burden of helpless tears that rolled down to the convulsive mouth. The hand that had held the cup remained upstretched as though petrified.

'Yer all right, now, yer all right,' crooned the low voice at her side. 'It's a good greet ye need, maybe; but just keep thinkin' that yer all right.'

David, gaunt against the white window, sat motionless on his chair. The suspense of the moment had his heart at breaking-point and he dared not stir. His body was cloddish, and any movement would have been a clumsy betrayal.

He waited thus while Mr Adair, whose actions seemed practised and sure, went out of the room and opened a press door in the lobby. There was a clinking of glass and the murmuring prattle of 'Yer all right' until he returned and put a medicine-glass to her lips. 'There now. Yer Adam's apple's no' done yet. Ay, it's a nasty stuff.'

Lips so immobile a moment before now screwed to a bloodless pucker.

'Oh, it's hideous,' she groaned.

'Naebody wanted ye to take it,' her husband grumbled, feeling it safe to expand so much; 'if ye'd only kept quiet.'

For the first time he turned toward the window.

'She takes turns when she's been excited.'

'Well, shouldn't we keep her quiet now?' David managed to ask. 'I'm so sorry. I'd no idea . . . '

'She'll be fine in a moment or two.'

'There's really no need for excitement, you know,' the young fellow went on.

'No, no, son, I know that,' Mrs Adair's voice broke through. 'Something just comes over me.'

'Ay, something comes over her, like.'

'But perhaps I should be going.' David thrust himself to his feet. 'You'll be tired.'

'No.'

'No, she's all right. Just you do the talking and I'll heat a hot-water bottle for her feet.'

David was left standing by the bed. With her head slightly to one side and her eyes almost closed she seemed to be resting. But beads of perspiration lay on her brow and her lips were blue. At this close range she appeared to have been wrung out by pain.

'Please don't get excited, dear,' he whispered. In the poignant urge of the moment he felt his appeal as pandering to a wild desire within him for self-sacrifice. 'Remember how you have suffered already and keep yourself for Jessie. We'll look after you.' He was bending over her, his voice soft as a caress. 'Jessie told me she's worried. She thinks she hasn't been good enough to you, and now she wants to make up for it. . . .

'So she'll come back and then we'll all be together and have jolly times. . . .

'I've got it all planned. I've got a good job and can easily afford it . . . .'

At each of his pauses he heard her breath as a gentle hiss through clenched teeth.

'Just think of that! We'll have a nice bright house and a maid to help Jessie. And I was telling her we'd arrange mirrors in your room so that you'd see into the garden, perhaps, and into other parts of the house, maybe. And you'd hear the birds in the mornings and listen to the chatter going on in the house. Now, surely there's nothing to make you ill in all this? Cheer up, won't you?'

Her eyes had opened slowly to his last words and the light of the window was reflected to a pin-point in their sombre depths. When he stopped and a slow smile overspread his face, the eyelids quivered and gradually fell, shutting him out again. But the lips, though a tooth kept a corner indrawn, were smooth and peaceful now.

'God bless you!' she murmured, far away.

He went into the kitchen and whispered to Mr Adair that she was asleep.

'She'll only have closed her eyes,' he was told. 'She'll be wantin' a rest.'

'Can I do anything for you in the house?' he then asked.

'There's naethin' I know of.'

'Yes, there is,' David said, noticing a bucket of refuse piled high under the sink. 'I'll take this down to the midden.'

'Ach, Kate'll take that when she comes.'

'But it's full. It must go now. No, I'll take it.'

Without more ado he gripped the bucket and went out.

When he came back Mr Adair was sitting on the bed's edge and the hot-water bottle was under the blankets at her feet.

She was smiling wanly. 'Such a thing for you to do! Kate would have taken it in the morning.'

'That's nothing,' he replied brightly. 'I'm so glad you're better. You look better. She'll be all right, won't she, Mr Adair?'

'I'll be fine,' she assured him, and smiled again.

'I telt her she'd be all right,' Mr Adair said with emphasis unusual for him.

It had been done on a sudden inspiration to make things right for Jessie when she returned—as she must return, whatever happened. Who, however, could have foreseen such an effect as that torture of joy upon the woman? And who, having seen it, would not have an aching desire to make the joy a real prospect for her? That which was started as a ruse to entrap Jessie was now by the involution of his own feelings changed into a passionate resolve as he set out for Langside Road.

'I'll make her do it—I'll make her!' he whispered to himself, using the words as faggots upon his inward fire. He would not leave her; he would not send her back alone; she would be made to do this thing he willed. 'I'll make her—I'll make her do it!' And wasn't she the prize? Wouldn't he have her just the same and his desire for her be another side of the happiness if he brought them all together under one roof?

But all this came from the anger of despair, for he was heading towards Langside Road prepared for defeat. She knew nothing of the ecstasy that had exhausted her mother. She had not the imaginative vigour to understand even if she were told. Elemental roots of feeling were never stirred in her otherwise than by the animal processes of her sex. Rather, she would fight with all her energy against this decent act whose moral principle complicated life and impinged upon her freedom.

When he arrived she was sitting at the window hemming a new dress for her holidays, and on the table were scattered pieces of lace and ribbons, strips of fragile cloth, bobbins and threads, the contents of a workbasket he had given her shortly after she had come to Langside. These she now gathered with a sweep of her hands and tidied away.

'I thought I wasn't to see you tonight!' she cried. 'What fun!'

'I got finished sooner than I expected and hurried along,' he said.

Mrs Watson was safely retired to the kitchen. She would stay there, discreetly quiet, until it was time for supper. Then she would make a warning noise with the kitchen door and cross over with a tray of tea or milk and scones or biscuits. Secure in their seclusion, David and Jessie faced each other.

His lips were hot: the passion of his kisses thrilled her. A few minutes ago she had been sitting sewing, aloof from everyone, at a high window in a tall building, cool as the evening light in the sky. Now his kisses challenged all she had been thinking.

She had been musing as she sewed. The sunlight had slanted across the roof-tops opposite and then upon a window that had broadcast bright rays upon her table and lap. From her chair was visible a strip of the Queen's Park, where rich green trees climbed to an azure sky. Langside Road itself had glints of green leaf and grass, and overhead some frail clouds were alight from the unseen sun. It was a pleasant place which inevitably moved her to dreams of places pleasanter still.

She had been thinking, too, of how much more efficient she was in meeting people than she used to be. Her fear of herself had been her besetting sin in the old days. She had never trusted herself to hold a boy, so that when she was going with Jimmy McIndoe she had known Francis, and when it was Francis she had known Jacky, and when it was Jacky she had palavered with others. But when David came she had not bothered about anyone else. Jimmy Crane of the Ringside Players, for instance: he had given a few unmistakable signs, but she had kept him strictly to the business of playacting. As she had grown fonder of David and his way of living she had become less and less disposed to waste her time elsewhere.

But now—now that she had given up all thought of anyone and everyone for him—now there was this plan of his before her like a terror. It was monstrous. No man in the world was worth it. As an idea it was utterly unworkable. And in the process of its being found unworkable every decent notion he had of her would be destroyed. The impossible thing was that she could not explain all this to him. She had to invent excuses that were easier targets for his powder and shot.

Something in his manner warned her; the subject filled her mind.

Holding her gently he whispered:

'Darling, I've decided!'

'On what, dear?'

'We must get married soon. I can't go on any longer without you.'

'But, my dear, how wonderful! Do you really mean it?'

'Every word!'

'I mean, will we manage?'

'Somehow, we'll have to.'

'When can it be, then?'

'Soon—perhaps next month.'

'David! And where will it be?'

'We'll see about that. We'll have to talk to Elizabeth.'

'My dear.'

'We'll easily get a house if we—we don't go to Cornfoot Avenue. Perhaps it would be best to leave Elizabeth there meantime.'

'We can stay away out in the country, perhaps?' she suggested breathlessly.

He nodded. 'Yes, possibly. And I've been thinking, dear, we'd easily get another door made into the house so that your folk could be really quite separate from us. That would be the better way for your father, perhaps. He'd have more freedom and so would we.'

He spoke as though it were all definitely fixed. Yet there was a good compromise in this. Some days ago, when he had first made the proposal, he would have thought the scheme vitiated by such a concession. But now he must do all he could. He faced her brightly, his whole attitude showing that he expected her glad approval.

But on a backward movement of her head, and a cold

glitter entering her eye, his face darkened. Impetuously he caught her in his arms again and kissed her urgently.

'I know the idea didn't appeal to you at first, dearest, but honestly, I'd almost forgotten. Never mind, it wouldn't appeal to any girl at the beginning. I sometimes think I hate it myself. But it can't be helped. It's one of these things we must do. So don't try to shield me by refusing. Trust me, darling; I'm game for anything for your sake.'

'Well, don't think of it again, for my sake.' Her voice was dull and loveless, but he went on as though he had not heard.

'When parents are healthy and prosperous a girl wants to leave them and start on her own. But just because your folk are unhealthy and inactive, just because they're poor and have forgotten what happiness is, just because they are becoming quite helpless, we must take them.

'You know, dear, I'm an ass, for I'm scared of mentioning something to you. It's so fashionable just now to despise it that I'm scared of it. But, Jessie, this thing is our duty. . . .

'Not duty in the ridiculous sense of sacrificing ourselves to something we don't approve. Obviously it's not that, for this that we must do is not customary. But duty in the sense that decent behaviour is our duty. That's the only definition of the word in the modern world.

'Personally, it's my duty. I can't take you away and keep you to myself when these two people need you so much. The thought of them in their helplessness would come charging into the peace of every hour—we'd have no real peace. . . .'

Her head had rested on his shoulder, his cheek touching her hair. He was gazing at the window, dreamy-eyed, the reasonableness of his argument bringing its own conviction to his heart apart from what Jessie would say or do.

'If you knew how cruel they had been to me for years and years, you'd never suggest such things. I'd do my duty all right, as you know, but it's no use. And, in any case, they would not come. You don't understand at all.'

'Oh yes, I do. And we'll make them come. I know they'll come. That's why I suggest we should have separate doors and separate sides of the house. You'd have a maid, and between you you'd manage both sides easily. The maid could sleep in their portion, and so we'd be entirely alone at night. You wouldn't need to see your father for days on end, unless you wanted.'

'But why not keep them where they are, then? We could visit them. Give them a maid, if you're so solicitous. It would be better that way. Huh!' she exploded, seeing the inadequacy of this.

His voice continued evenly. 'The object, darling, is their happiness. You left them because—well, because they were cruel to you. They didn't mean to be cruel, as we've since agreed, but they simply hadn't the vitality to be kindly. Kindliness is an activity of the heart. It means definite action. Cruelty is different. We can be cruel in a negative sort of way; inaction is sometimes damnably cruel. Sometimes people are so listless and weak that they can't be bothered taking any interest. That's your folk's sort of cruelty. Why, then, when you resented it in them so much, should you want us to practise it?'

'Oh, you don't understand—'

'It wasn't so much the bodily inconveniences, the arduous life, the rows about clothes that you resented, darling; it was the mental cruelty caused by their lack of interest. But think: how could they in their state of health be active? They didn't *mean* to be cruel. You wanted to be petted, admired, loved; you wanted that natural fuss made of you by your own folk which makes you feel important and attractive. But you were asked to forego all that and instead expend your kindliness on them. Of course, you didn't see it that way. You could hardly be expected to. You only saw them as careless and crude toward you. Is that not so?'

'Oh, what's the use of talking?' she sighed, and, slowly withdrawing from him, she moved toward the window. With her back to him she continued, 'No, no, no; you've got it all wrong. That is not so. I didn't want to be petted and admired—by them. I wanted to be left alone so that I could live my own life. And that's what I want today.'

She stood erect, her heels close together, the palms of her hands turned inwards against her skirt. Occasionally her head quivered and the even line of hair at the nape of her neck was ever so slightly reverberant. She seemed to be standing still for his inspection and at the same time enforcing a silence to give effect to her words. His temper rose as he looked at her, slim, graceful, strong, the mistress of a quiet room in which she had neither to cook nor tidy. She was free to sew and read and be waited upon by an elderly woman. She had gained this ease by escaping from her parents and depending on his weekly envelope, slipped as casually as possible into her strong young fingers.

'But no one is entitled to live one's own life with no thought of others,' he broke into the silence harshly, striding forward.

Her gaze was fixed on the roof of the tenement building opposite, and as he approached her only response was a deliberate narrowing of the eyes as though she had been struck. Resenting this, he continued in a bullying tone:

'Don't you realize that?'

The eyes narrowed still more and a red lip was blanched by the grip of a tooth.

'For God's sake speak!' he cried.

'What is there for me to say?' She turned imploringly, in injured innocence. 'Why should you always roar at me when this subject comes up?'

'You were trying to aggravate me. So now there can be no discussion. All I have said has gone for nothing—made absolutely no impression on you.'

'How could it, David? It's all so—wrong. You're so stupidly optimistic. You'd waste our lives for the sake of those whose lives are wasted already. They never bothered about me. And we've so little time—oh, you don't understand.'

Disappointment wrenched him back violently to his former self in which he had perceived all this as his justification for leaving her. Before all this excitement began, before all his lengthy explaining, he had known the result was to be this. But during those brief moments, when he had persuaded himself by his arguments, he had seen the utter degradation of his own position as well as hers, and now the integrity of the woman in Black Street, whose case he had been fighting, loomed up in his mind like a rock. What a fool he had been to think that any lies of his could bring brightness to that woman's life, or that any condescension on his part was going to alter her destiny! He had mocked her with his idle impudent talk, embarrassed her frail body to exquisite pain; but her dignity remained, she loomed up now in his mind like a rock—unassailable.

He held himself in control, and at last, when she gave up her pose of wounded virtue, he spoke, in pleasant tones:

'Isn't it curious that two people can see a thing so differently?'

'It is. But I see all you see, and knowing more than you do, know you to be all wrong.'

She didn't dream of how much he knew. He smiled at the confident toss of her head.

His mind was cooled by the thought that he could not injure the woman in Black Street whatever he did. She was beyond his hurt, for suffering was her estate. His voice was once more tender when he spoke.

'Maybe I am wrong. You should know. I just remember the conditions of the house as I saw it once. It was only for your sake, I assure you—to see you do the right thing. I'm not keen.'

She looked at him quickly.

'Well, do take my word for it,' she pleaded.

'I will—now. Unless you'd like to take me to Black Street one evening and we could compare notes afterwards?'

'Oh, certainly.'

But her cheeks burned. This had been a contingency she had dreaded; yet for the moment she had to agree with no reserve.

Watching her closely, he saw that she was moved.

'Well?' he persevered, 'when can we go? Tomorrow?'

'Tomorrow? But I'm supposed to be in Dundee. And a letter is just away, isn't it?'

'When, then?'

'Later. There's lots of time. Next week, perhaps.'

'A week today, let us say?'

'Yes. But let's have no more of this just now. I'm sick of it.'

She sat down on the bed's edge and he bent down and touched her hair with his lips. She looked up and her face was close to his. Smiling, his eyes cleared of all temper, he murmured, 'You dear!' and kissed her. His thought went forward wildly to the chance he now had, in this quiet room, of giving himself the escape of satiety from so much yearning and so many irresolute desires.

He knew, when he thought of it afterwards, that the final defeat of this night had been the result of his own training. She had looked wonderingly at him, but remained cautious toward his hints and impetuous appeals, believing them to be but some new and transient folly from this strange character. Her inaction, therefore, and her gentleness in warding him off, in a mood of bland and loving misunderstanding, were her tribute to his past comradeship.

Had he been quick enough to grasp the situation then, he would have smothered the impression with a decent regretting and gone home. But the strain of so many conflicting emotions and of such contending forces as mother-love and the flesh and spoil of youth had tired him, and now that he was beaten, his moral zest permanently impaired, one overwhelming desire swept him on. Again and again she pulled him up at their accepted boundaries, albeit lovingly and with signs that she feared to misinterpret his meaning.

But there was no mistaking his meaning, and as the minutes were ticked away by a tiny clock on the mantelpiece, around which a dustiness of shadow was gathering, she realized further that this was no sudden breaking upon his restraint, no temporary lapse in his respect for her. It was a calculated thing, vitally associated with the harsh and wordy clash which had preceded it. He was now seeking something which she had once offered and which he had masterfully refused. His refusal then made his seeking now an omen of dismay.

The realization convulsed her. She seemed suddenly unmanageably frail and about to break under the strain of her sobbing. He mistook her tears as those of despair and strove to comfort her, in the only way his sense could guide him now, by going on to achieve his end. But her sobs were of the bitterness of failure and out of the very strength of her nature and not its weakness. Her love for him was turned to hate at this first sign of danger. She might have been the victim of an assault, so moistly and wanly did she push him from her, the feeble force of her arms a measure of her body's inaction toward him.

But it would not do to let him know she had discovered him. She wanted time to think and plan. If she uttered now the accusing words that burned her brain he would go away and never return. She would then be stranded.

She succeeded in smiling through her tears, lighting a promise for him in her eyes, and with her lips beseeching relief from present pain. He passed out of her room at last, after they had sat at the window, the supper tray between them, like an animal that has been beaten away by random blows in the dark.

Two days later he got a letter from Black Street. The handwriting on the envelope had puzzled him, and when he saw the address he was surprised. Somehow he had not expected the man Adair to have such an excellent fist. The words were roundly, smoothly formed, recognizably of the penmanship of the older generation, with that trace of copperplate exactitude surviving in the general impression of speed. The message was brief:

> My Dear Boy,
>   Mrs Adair has been thinking of what you told us the last time you were here and she wants to see you again about it. Do you think you could spare a few minutes some day soon? She will be pleased to see you and won't keep you long.
>
>   Yours faithfully,
>   William Adair

He did not want to go. He had lost the sureness of his attitude toward the woman, and in the instability of his mood he was afraid of her. But he urged himself to face the ordeal in the evening, and when once at her bedside found that the impression he had left was ample to cover his deficiencies now. Mrs Adair looked with her old directness, but with warmth; the feeling that her eyes were clutching at him was renewed, but he found himself steadied instead of challenged.

'I hope you haven't been put out coming over so soon?' she asked. 'But I've been very worried.'

'Worried? Did you get over your turn all right?'

She waved that aside. 'Yes. It's what you told me about. You mustn't do it.'

'Mustn't?'

'No, no, no. It would never do. Have you said any more

about it to Jessie?'

'No, but she's written again about it."

'Now, are you sure?'

She doubted his statement, but not his essential truthfulness. She was convinced of his goodness of heart, but she knew Jessie with a searing accuracy.

'Yes,' he insisted, but his voice was timid.

'Well', she sighed, making up her mind to let this pass, 'you'll just go away and think no more about it. Jessie and you'll have enough to do looking after yourselves. We'll manage fine. The Lord's always provided for us yet. But Jessie's no' the girl to do things like that. I thought I'd better just send for you and tell you that.'

He marvelled at her courage.

'You mean to say,' he asked her, 'that she is not really serious about you and her father coming to stay with us?'

She lifted her hand slowly as he spoke and let it fall again weariedly.

'She may be serious just now, my boy; but once we were together it would never do. She may be serious, but don't force her. You tell her *you* don't want it to happen. That's the best way. Then she won't think I've warned you.'

'Oh, she wouldn't think that.'

'Well, you never know.'

She looked at him steadfastly for a moment and smiled. She showed that the thing was settled and done with.

'It was so good of you to think about it,' she murmured; 'you're a good boy.'

'It was only what anyone would have suggested. It was so obvious.'

'Ah well,' she nodded, reserving her reasons for thinking otherwise, 'just you run away now and not let me keep you. I've taken up too much of your time as it is. And forget about that altogether.'

Mr Adair, who had been in the kitchen all this while,

now entered the room. He was in his shirtsleeves and in his hand he carried a fork. A dish-towel was thrown over his shoulder. 'Are ye stayin' for a cup o' tea?' he asked.

But David excused himself, and nodding a regretful promise to Mrs Adair's final 'Mind, now!' he hastened away.

Every time he met Jessie thereafter the contest which began on that decisive night at her lodgings was renewed. The thought of it absorbed him in the daytime, and at night he gave himself up to its purpose, which became more resolute the more she resisted. But in spite of all his guile and the urgency of his love-making he failed. That which he had once known to await him plenteously in the future was now beyond his reach. She had discovered his intention. She saw it confirmed in his loss of interest in ordinary things, his facile agreement to arrangements he would once have pondered. The intensity of his ardour in such circumstances was a sign of desertion.

It was nothing to her to know that in any case they must now part. She had no need for sacrifice as he had for triumph in the culmination of their friendship. She viewed his failing without magnanimity and closed against him instinctively, as she had closed against others before him. The thought that she had tricked him, in and out of their love-making, with deceits and exaggerations, did not trouble her beyond bringing the inevitable regret that once again she had failed. Already, although they continued their walks and fondling, he was discarded in her mind and she was searching out her next lover. She was keeping herself for her real lover, whenever he might arrive. Her warmth for David was withdrawn as though it had been a flow in her veins, and he found that her flesh was cold and mortal as her selfishness.

The day they had fixed for their visit to Black Street

arrived, and in the evening they walked the roads above Clarkston and ultimately to the grassy hollow beyond 'Hedges'. Their talk was of the idlest, of office and shop, of people they knew and had known, and of holidays they had had in days before they knew each other. Recollections of this sort helped their independence. They were retreating into the past, to reclaim an individuality that had been surrendered when their affair began. David sensed that she had divined his intention. He realized that she was too ready to agree to any material proposal he made, too careless or indifferent toward what had once been of great moment. Of their holidays next month she had grown as reticent as he was, possibly sharing his shame at leaving a memory of more deceit than was necessary.

There was a difference, however, between idle hypocrisy and the purposeful plan to get her home. She knew he wanted her back at Black Street, where she would be safely anchored when he forsook her. She could have foretold his method, which began to show one Friday night after she had taken, without a word, the weekly envelope which helped with her rent. He was tender and soft voiced as he gathered her to his arms and in a minute was assailing the boundaries, with tempestuous kisses and caresses. But she was firm and resolute and at length he gave it up.

His voice was tender still:

'We're wasting an awful time,' he whispered. It was as though his passion drove him to decisions. He must have her: she must relent. 'Aren't we?'

'Yes,' she agreed.

'Hadn't we better get married, then, as soon as we can?'

She wanted to laugh. If she had laughed she would have exploded the whole sordid business. She should have told him to his face that he was a liar, that he was like all the rest. But she could not break the suspense of the moment. She was held bound.

'If you go back now,' he said, 'and tell your folk that you are home to be married, that will help things on. You can say you are going to work in your old shop until we're ready. And you can talk about getting them a housekeeper when you leave. That will keep them sweet.'

She replied with no hesitation, 'Very well, I'll go next week.'

For a moment her eyes filled with tears. But as his gaze became questioning they cleared and she smiled as she murmured, 'It won't be long, will it?'

This was a little more than acting; it was the last, broken word of their love.

'No.'

She got out her notepaper and wrote as he bid her in a letter to her parents. She had fixed up with her old employers, she told them, and would start work in Glasgow on Monday week. She would be home on Saturday.

He went away to post the letter to his friend in Dundee, and with it he enclosed a note saying that this was to be the last. His fingers held the envelope as it was poised in the shoot, and then he heard it fall with a slither out of his reach. That had been a little ceremony in private. It would never happen again.

Over Victoria Road, where he was, and extending beyond the green heights of the Queen's Park, the sky was cobbled by cirrus cloud flushed with pink. There was quietness and peace in that far-away sky. But Victoria Road was busy with people flocking from the park, where minstrels were entertaining the crowd. The light and colour of the girls' dresses gave a gaiety to the scene that had little confirmation in the faces of many of the girls and seemed at violence with the peace of the sky. Some of the girls looked at him coldly, ready to disdain the slightest flicker of interest and disdainful when none was shown. These were the vulnerable ones. Others who passed, full of their own interests, were young and lissom, and he looked on them as he might on a meadowland filled again with the promise of spring. For this was the end and a new beginning: he was free! He was back again to where he had been when Clifford and he had met Jessie and Bessie Fowlis on their memorable night in town. He was back again to a consideration of Clifford's outlook, and prepared to believe that his own fussiness over feelings and impressions was a weakness which Clifford was justified in despising. Jessie was much nearer to Clifford than to him, and all his elaborate tenderness for her and her mother might just as well have been spent upon Clifford.

And there was Elizabeth. With her there had been some permanent damage done. She would never forget the impression of this affair, tentative and vague as his intimation of it had been. She saw in Jessie an estimate of his desires and a forecast of his destiny, let it be Jessie or someone else. He would never be quite on equal terms with Elizabeth again.

She did not understand, of course, what had happened. He had had intentions at once too base and too exalted for her to understand.

He wandered into the park and mingled with the crowd near the minstrels. There was the smell of cut grass in the air, which brought a vivid recollection of the grassy hollow beyond 'Hedges'. The people around him seemed too much at ease in this place where the ground was trampled bare and children scampered and park attendants moved with wary eyes. What a debased and empty life it was when compared with the excitement of the grassy hollow, where no one ever came to interrupt and the grass was rich and springy! But he was one of the crowd now; he might as well be here as anywhere else. And there must be a secret trafficking gone on here that wasn't seen on the surface; a trafficking which led, soon or late, to grassy hollows and to secret sweetness he only guessed at. This was Clifford's crowd, and he must mix with it again until he learned the movement of its unseen life and shared in its inner meaning.

On the following Thursday night Jessie was sitting up very late. Mrs Watson was in bed, and the silence in the house and in the street below was absolute. It started a ringing in her ears so that she shook her head irritably and for a second afterwards the room swung about her. She was tired and longing for her pillow; but, though everything was done, she was afraid to go to bed and lose herself in sleep. She wanted something else to do that would prolong, be she ever so wearied, this sensation of acting for herself in a secret plan. But everything she could possibly do was done. Her bags were packed and strapped, all save the small attaché-case into which she had to throw her nightdress-case and brush and comb in the morning. Audaciously she had arranged that Jimmy Crane should call for her bags and take them to the station. David would call for her in the evening to take her over to Black Street. But by that time she would be well on her way to London. On Monday she would be reporting at a theatre, and who was there to sneer at her if she was starting in the profession as a chorus girl in a musical play? Jimmy Crane had praised her pluck and promised that he too would try for a job in London.

She kept repeating to herself, 'I shan't see David again,' but it was fading in spite of her. She was ceasing to be incredulous of it. She had experienced this thing so often that she knew not whether she lived or acted the regret that was in the words. The very thought of a new love was so familiar as to be scarcely worth while. It was this daring adventure that was new. It at least was real. And so exciting was the prospect of it that she dallied when she should have been in bed, unconvinced that all arrangements for so drastic a change could be complete. This at least she had not done before. In a life such as she had lived nothing ever happened. Love came and went and no one but herself knew or cared. The cave-like shop had swallowed up the years so that now they were dates indistinguishable in their sameness. Now she would see that hateful shop no more.

By going away to London she would make a break that must bring some change. No one there would know of her or find out anything she wished to keep to herself. But for how long would that last? Something always occurred to foil her in the end. She saw boy after boy react in the same way and then came trickery and a parting. All she wanted was to be allowed to live decently. Her lips tightened as she thought of what she could have done for David.

The reflection that she might have won had she agreed to his suggestion then pierced her decisive mood, and she decided, tolerantly, as though for nothing else to do, to consider it. It gave her the cue, as it were, to admit that perhaps she had been pretty selfish hopping off and leaving F. and M. David had seen that. And he had learned from that to fear her selfishness in other ways. She was able to reason it all out from their point of view. She saw what was the usual thing to do and why it was usual. The emotions that stirred David to sacrifice were known to her. But, whereas he was overwhelmed by these emotions, she saw the dark deterioration that followed any yielding to them. She was selfish only because the inertia of other people made her demands seem so. Her selfishness was exposed by their extreme and unfair need of her. Millions must go through life equally selfish as she, but because of congenial circumstances never discovered. Had but David seen that! How she would have served him, worshipped him, bewitched him! Had she been well provided and well cared for, ah then, there would have been no talk of her selfishness. Nor had there been when they were together in the grassy hollow or on the sides of Loch Lomond or Loch Long under the pine trees. The lips tightened again and then broke into a sneer that lingered long at the corners. When she reached this point she could see but one thing, her capacity to love, and she was trained to believe this capacity the most sacred in the world of men. David had known of it and found it insufficient. Then he had tried to betray it. She did not understand that.

The silence was getting on her nerves. There was something immoral in staying up aimlessly so long. She would go to bed.